S0-ARO-316

Rochester Public Library
Rochester, New Hampshire

DISCARDED

to be Mona

Also by Kelly Easton

Aftershock

Walking on Air

The Life History of a Star

Margaret K. McElderry Books

to be Mona

Kelly Easton

Margaret K. McElderry Books
New York London Toronto Sydney

Margaret K. McElderry Books

An imprint of Simon & Schuster Children's Publishing Division
1230 Avenue of the Americas, New York, New York 10020

This book is a work of fiction. Any references to historical events, real
people, or real locales are used fictitiously. Other names, characters,
places, and incidents are products of the author's imagination, and any
resemblance to actual events or locales or persons, living or dead, is
entirely coincidental.
Copyright © 2008 by Kelly Easton
All rights reserved, including the right of reproduction in whole or in part
in any form.

Book design by Debra Sfetsios
The text for this book is set in Helvetica Lt Std.
Manufactured in the United States of America
10 9 8 7 6 5 4 3 2 1
Library of Congress Cataloging-in-Publication Data
Easton, Kelly.
To be Mona / Kelly Easton.—1st ed.
p. cm.
Summary: High school senior Sage tries to hide her mentally ill mother
and get a popular football player to go out with her, but eventually
she realizes that abandoning her real friends and letting herself be
manipulated by others does not make her feel better after all. Includes
author's note about bipolar disorder and abusive relationships.
Includes bibliographical references.
ISBN-13: 978-1-4169-0054-2 (hardcover)
ISBN-10: 1-4169-0054-3 (hardcover)
[1. Mothers and daughters—Fiction. 2. Manic-depressive illness—Fiction.
3. Mental illness—Fiction. 4. Self-confidence—Fiction. 5. Identity—
Fiction. 6. Dating (Social customs)—Fiction. 7. Single parent families—
Fiction. 8. High schools—Fiction. 9. Schools—Fiction.] I. Title.
PZ7.E13155To 2008
[Fic]—dc22
2007049402

For my friends
Jean Brown and Lori Halloran

Many thanks to Karen Wojtyla,
Sarah Payne, and Emma Dryden of
Margaret K. McElderry Books.

WAL-MART

Hypothetical question

CONSIDER yourself a color.
What would you be? Red? Blue? Tangerine or teal?
How are you dressed?
Did you *really* pick your own clothes?
Are you wearing a label, someone's stamp on you?
Whose name is it?
What does it mean?
Does it tell you who you are?

SAGE

I'D RATHER BE WEARING GREEN PLAID and pink and yellow polka dots. . . . I'd rather have a volcanic zit bubbling on my nose. . . . I'd rather be locked in a small jail cell with a pissing camel, an angry cobra, and a hungry lion . . . than be where I am right now, standing next to Mona *Perfect* Simms in front of the 468 students of Stafford High.

No one told me that running for class president meant that I was up for public dissection, that kids would draw extra body parts on my posters, write obscenities on my banner, and change my pep song to include references to my weight. No one informed me that it was not about making changes at the school, but a popularity contest, like homecoming queen.

And DEFINITELY, no one confided that we would have to stand on the stage like this and hear the vote count read aloud:

Absent—2

Mona Simms—374

Vernon Goldburg—70

Sage Priestly (ME!)—22

That *22* is every member of the Thespian Society minus me. I voted for Vernon.

Mona whips around, her blonde hair floating, like in a commercial; she's too beautiful for reality TV.

She cranks Vern's hand like she's pumping a flat tire. Vern's double-jointed. He does this move, his right arm looped through his left elbow. Everyone laughs. Except Mona. It might give her smile lines.

I am standing apart on the stage like a kid peeing her pants at the kindergarten pageant. My body feels like a giant pillar, only I'm not holding anything up. A pillar with nothing to support has a tendency to topple.

Roger Willis jumps up and down in the audience, going "Mo-na. Mo-na. Mo-na." My mouth waters like he's cherry cough drops and I've got a cold.

Finally, Mona turns from Vern and offers me a charming shrug, as if to say, *Sorry, loser.* She grabs my hand and tugs me forward, hugs me for a century or two. "Good job," she whispers to my hair.

"Good job" is like giving a quarter to an Iraq War veteran with his legs blown off.

Twenty-two votes. *Good job.*

Principal Chard (like the vegetable) calls into the microphone: "Mona Simms, Student Body President."

Applause. Applause for Mona.

"Well, kiddo." Vern gives me a squeeze. "Back to obscurity."

I force a smile. My lip catches on my braces. "I'm sorry I made you do this."

"Anything for a friend." Which pretty much sums up Vern.

Chard leads us offstage. We no longer belong. Mona stands in the center and waves, little parade hand, mechanical.

My armpits are sweaty and my pants feel too tight. I crave chocolate in a big way. And, in this moment, it strikes me why I hate Mona so much, why I have hated her since third grade. It's because more than anything else, I want to be her. I want so much to be Mona.

VERN

"**BEAR WITH ME**." Walter wipes the table with his napkin for the fiftieth time.

"I'm bearing." I shove a tortilla chip into salsa.

"You wake up one morning and everything's changed. Your mom isn't your mom. Your room isn't your room. The things you liked to do—robotics, Pokémon, skateboarding, physics—no longer give you a kick."

"Physics has never given me a kick."

"Strange protuberances appear on your body. Hair sprouts. You don't recognize your own bedroom. I mean, there's a poster with a cocker spaniel on it, for God's sake. Things that used to be normal, like toothpaste and yogurt, seem poisonous and radioactive. It's as if a priest has sprung out of your floor like a tree, and he's giving you a sermon about your life, only it's not your life. You're getting a guilt trip for someone else's life!"

"Where did the priest come from?" I finish the last chip. "I mean, priests don't just grow out of the floor. Are you taking your medication?"

"The priest comes from reality."

"There's no priest in my reality."

"Okay, Vern. A rabbi. A rabbi grows out of the floor."

"You aren't taking your medication, are you?"

Lila, the waitress, appears with a fresh basket of chips. For years, Sage and I have tried to figure out how old she is. She could be eighty, but her makeup . . . fake eyelashes, red lipstick. Looking at her, you'd swear you were in a bowling alley cocktail lounge instead of a Mexican restaurant. "You want to order?" she says.

"What's the point?" Walter's glasses are so thick, his eyes are magnified. "Food doesn't help anything."

Lila yawns. "No point."

"I'll have a black bean burrito, extra guacamole and sour cream," I tell her.

"Like always," she says.

"Walter'll have a taco."

"I guess this is Walter."

"You're a brain surgeon," Walter says.

"I'm going to spit in your food." She storms off.

"Did you notice her fingernails? They were, like, eight inches long," Walter says.

"They're fake."

"She sounds Russian. What's a Russian doing working in a Mexican restaurant?"

"Beats me."

"Where was I?"

"Your mom isn't your mom anymore?"

"I used to love my mom. I thought her suffering was touching. But this mom is like a weight on me."

"That's because you're a teenager."

"My point exactly. We've grown up. I'm not me anymore. You're not you. I mean, you used to giggle, Vern. You were all skinny and flexible. Now, you look kind of buff, if you want to know the truth."

"I've been lifting weights."

"That's what I mean. You're not you."

"Maybe that's not a bad thing. Like, I don't think a girl has been interested in me in all my years of high school. But the other day, when I got off the stage, Cassandra Parks rushes up to me and plants a wet one on my mouth! With a tongue! A tongue, Walter. Randomly."

"That's good, right? A tongue is good."

"Cassandra is a babe in this fabricated kind of way. But her voice . . . Her voice makes me feel like there are bugs crawling under my skin."

"I saw a foreign film where ants crawl out of this guy's hand."

"Let's try to stay on topic. Me."

"Here's your burrito." Lila brings the food.

"Thanks. You're a doll," I tell her.

"And *your* taco."

"Did you spit on it?" Walter examines it.

"Why bother?"

Walter pushes the taco toward me. "Why did you run for president anyway?"

"Because Sage asked me."

"Do you do anything she asks?"

"Pretty much. I'm her guardian angel. I've been taking care of her since she was four. I even saved her life a couple of times. And because . . . I am madly in love with her."

"So, no Cassandra Parks."

"I don't know. Maybe I should. I mean, Sage thinks of me as this big brother slash next-door neighbor. If she saw me with someone, maybe she'd think of me as date material. What do you think?"

"I don't know. Sage doesn't seem like the other girls. She's completely clueless, which is good. Because what the other girls are clued into is nasty stuff, like celebrity mating habits. Sage is real."

And she's got a thing for Roger Willis, I want to tell him, but I don't want to murder his appetite any further. "Eat your taco."

"Is Sage's mom still a wacko?" he asks.

"Totally. One day she's pleasant and seminormal, the next I can hear her screaming her head off at all hours. She makes *you* look normal. Eat your taco."

Reluctantly, he takes a bite. "This is pretty good."

"I'm supposed to be applying to colleges and planning my future, and all I can think about is Sage."

"You know what you need?"

"I don't mind if you swallow before you talk."

"Seriously." Lettuce drops out of his mouth.

"What?"

"A pet monkey."

"You are so random."

"They can cook their own meals and do chores. I saw one on TV that could knit. You gotta put it in a diaper, though. They are not into potty training."

SAGE

THAT DAY, ON STAGE, Vern said, "Back to obscurity." He was *so* right. Since the election, I've gone invisible again. Maybe that's a good thing. It's enough to see Mona's smug face on every piece of school-related propaganda and to hear her voice each morning, leading us in the Pledge of Allegiance like she's the world's cutest patriot.

If I'd been elected, I would've barred army recruiters from the campus and insisted on a new school menu with nouvelle cuisine. With Mona, it's "same ol', same ol'."

Since last year, everyone has gone on about colleges, but I don't have a clue. The counselor suggested community college, which means *aim low*. My grades aren't that bad, mostly Bs this year. No money for SATs.

I've got to get my act together! This afternoon, I'll call Johnson & Wales and ask them to send me an application. They've got a great program for chefs. Vern said there's a form to waive the application fee.

Everything is going so fast. I wanted to make this

year special, to finally shine, but I hardly have time to think, especially with the jogging and starving myself. There's a reason "diet" contains the word "die"! So far today, I have consumed one hard-boiled egg, three carrots, an orange, two celery sticks, and eight Wheat Thins. My stomach was groaning. My throat was constricted. I felt dizzy. But then I went to the Goldburg's, and Vern's sister, Sophie, made me a giant hot fudge sundae. She's so cute, I just couldn't say no.

Now the Goldburgs are off to temple, and I'm here, slogging through math and science like an elephant stuck in quicksand.

Anatomy homework: Hair   is   made   of the same stuff that   makes the nails, claws, and hooves of mammals, the   scales of reptiles, and the feathers of birds (and doesn't everyone want   to be   birds of a feather).

The space bar keeps sticking. I've had this laptop since freshman year, one of those birthday gifts Mom manages to pull out of a hat on holidays, like an annual proof of love.

That's another difference between me and everyone else: the technology thing. I do not have a TV (since Mom smashed it with a baseball bat), a cell phone, an iPod, or Internet. While everyone else is instant messaging, text messaging, and updating their profiles on

MySpace, I'm here in the day of the dinosaurs.

If we could just move somewhere where everyone else is poor—a trailer park in Alabama, say, where kids think it's a big thrill if they get Kool-Aid with dinner—I could fit in, maybe even be superior. But here, I am in the land of upward mobility. New York City and Boston, a stone's throw away, and I've never been to either (although Vern keeps promising me a day in Boston).

Hair is essentially   dead.

My own mousy locks have received some assistance from Cora at Cora's Elegance. She made me sweep the floor at the salon and clean the toilets as payment.

Cora said it would look like angels had dusted gold on my hair, but it looks more like they've driven over my head in trucks, leaving tire marks.

I've also thrown out all of the black clothes in my closet. I would have thrown out the gray, too, but I'd have nothing left. I filched a pink summer dress of Mom's. Hopefully, no Mom germs will rub off on me. I'm going to wear it to school tomorrow.

✗ ✗ ✗ ✗

Speaking of dresses, Mom just entered from stage left in her God-awful job-hunting dress, a baby blue number with raised white dots. She must have inherited it from some dead librarian. I will not be borrowing it.

She's going through drawer after drawer, looking for cigarettes, having some kind of conversation with herself at a sprinter's pace.

Aside from the dress, the other problem with Mom's "job search" is that this is a small town. Everyone knows that Mom is the model employee for all of two weeks. After that, come the "episodes."

a. Mom as a bank teller, tossing the money from her drawer up into the air, "to see the sky rain dollars."

b. Mom as a cleaning woman, dressing up in her employer's clothes and jewels, then lying on the couch with a magazine, a glass of champagne, and her feet up.

c. Mom in the day care center, crawling on all fours with the babies, eating their food, and dripping it down the front of her shirt. "I should have worn a bib," she told me, after she was "let go."

d. Mom's diatribes about God and Jesus, sex and sin, that she will spout to anyone who'll listen. Or, if she's in a good mood, about all the men who have been or are in love with her.

When people in this town see my mom, they cross

streets or leap into stores. If she manages to corner them and treat them to one of her monologues, there's the look of pure panic, the mumbled excuses, and then the escape.

I avoid going out with Mom at all costs. Even our cat, Selfish, steers clear, streaking out of any room she enters, or hiding in my lap like he is now.

✗ ✗ ✗ ✗

The facts of the matter:

Fact: Dad ran away when I was four, leaving only his plastic-wrapped suits in the closet, like black fish on hooks.

Fact: He has forgotten my existence.

Fact: Mom is into God. Very. And her God is not the sweet-faced Jesus or the wise man in the flowing gown. Her God is one of those fat bigots on TV who wants to bilk people of their money. (Before she was into God, she was into men, so this is an improvement.)

Fact: Mom's moods fly from one extreme to another. Some days it's like she's on amphetamines. Other days, she resembles a depressive pothead on sleeping pills.

Fact: We live next door to the Goldburgs: Peter, Miriam, Sophie, and Vern. They are my saviors.

Mrs. G. remembers when my mom used to wear makeup and drink iced tea, and sneak cigarettes with her on the porch so their husbands wouldn't find out. Mrs. G.'s explanation as to why my mom is such a lunatic is, "Your mom sure took it hard when your dad left."

Thirteen years later: not an excuse.

Vern is my best friend, although lately he's been weird toward me, suggesting wedding dates, and, well, dates.

✗ ✗ ✗ ✗

"Where are my cigarettes? Did you hide them?" Mom opens and closes drawers in search of the ubiquitous smoke.

"You mean your death sticks?"

"It's none of your business what sticks they are. They keep me thin. You wouldn't believe the day I had. I was applying for jobs, but there weren't any parking spaces. Everywhere I went I couldn't find a place. And in Newport. They have parking meters there, but I searched my purse and no quarters. It was like God didn't want me to find a job today. I need a smoke."

"You only have to feed the meters in the summer."

"I really can't *deal* without a smoke." She's pacing

like the tiger at the zoo. I always feel so sorry for the tiger in its small pen, running back and forth, wondering why its life purpose has been thwarted. To hunt. Mom the huntress. Hunting for a life.

"What's to deal *with*?"

"Unemployment. Single parenting. A sinful daughter."

"Sinful, how?" Just once, I'd like to commit the crime of which I'm accused.

"Well . . ." She peers around the kitchen for a sign of sin. "It's sinful that you spend all your time studying and none praying."

"Would you rather I be smoking dope or popping heroin?" I ask.

"I should homeschool you; that's what most Christians do. Jesus was homeschooled. In those days that's how they did things."

"And things turned out so stunningly well for him!"

I hate myself. That is the root of my problem. No one else at school seems to hate themselves, but I do. And I hate myself more when I am sarcastic to my mom. But I can't help it. I feel so mad sometimes.

She steps back like I hit her. I can tell she's about to pitch a fit, start throwing things or screaming, but then she finds one, a lone cigarette. Cigarette trumps tantrum. She rushes to the stove and lights it. "What did you do to your hair?" she says.

"Highlights."

"You look like a zebra."

"Like, a week ago."

"Who paid for it?"

"Cora did it for free."

"Cora never does anything for free."

"I cleaned the toilets. Okay?"

"Then you can clean the litter box. Right? You can clean up after the devil's spawn."

She goes into a rant about the cat, how my dad brought him home without even asking her, and now she's stuck with him (stuck with me). I cover Selfish's ears, so he won't be insulted.

I have memories of Mom and me when I was little. I remember picking pumpkins with her, taking them home, carving them, toasting and eating the seeds. I remember having plants in milk cartons along the windowsill and watching them grow. And Mom baking cookies, pies, and cakes, and me helping her. Maybe it's why I have such a thing for baking now.

I don't remember my dad at all. But, I remember *Mom*, when *he* was here.

"God will punish you if you're vain," Mom says.

The milk cartons are still there, filled with cigarette butts.

"He already has," I assure her, then I go to the closet and dig out a package of Chips Ahoy. I've already had the sundae. Why not sabotage myself completely?

WAL-MART

Hypothetical question

WHAT IF you were on *Survivor* or *American Idol*? Who would you be? The fat slob who sings like an angel? The chick who's cute but doesn't know how to move? The gay guy who's booted off the first week but gets his own show anyway? On what episode would you get voted out? Or would you win? Would that be you jumping up and down next to the campfire, pouring champagne into your mouth, living the myth? Hoping to be *something* in the land of nothing?

SAGE

WHO ARE YOU? is what a journal is asking. And what most people put in are lies. But I don't lie. That's the difference between me and everyone else: the Monas of the world, even the Roger Willises. I don't have a mask to hide behind.

Still, I don't mind stripping down for you, a notebook, a piece of paper. We are both made of trees. Peel off my bark. Chop off my branches (the crazy mom, the crappy house, the heavy body), then build me into something new. Make a mask of chicken wire, papier-mâché for the skin, a painted smile. Reinvention. To be Mona, my own version, so that life becomes LIFE instead of a dress rehearsal.

x x x x

"Next stop: the outlets," the bus driver calls out. I slide my notebook into my purse, trying not to wake the old lady who's fallen asleep on my shoulder. I thought I'd take the car this morning, but Mom had disappeared with it. No note. Just the coffee pot left on, and her coffee mug filled with cigarette butts.

I could've asked a friend, but I wanted to come alone.

When I go with the other girls, I feel like a dweeb with my empty wallet, pretending I don't want anything. And they always stop for coffee and lunch.

I am losing weight, finally staying on my die-t. It's like a drug, I guess. You lose some, you want to lose more. Bye-bye to poundage.

My next step is to try and be fashionable. Well, it's not really a step. A step would entail money. This is more of a fact-finding mission. Like, *What if?*

There's Prada, Dior, Roberto Cavalli, Coach, all the good stuff at the mall. I can fantasize about what I'll buy when I get a job, a paycheck.

Actually, I think the designer thing is a little weird. I mean, I know girls who spend three hundred dollars on sunglasses!

Still, it's inevitable. If you want to fit in, you wear the labels.

The bus pulls into the massive shopping center. I gently shake the lady awake. She stares at me with bright blue eyes. "Is it time to shop?"

"Yeah."

"Aren't you the prettiest thing I've ever seen," she says, which is nice, except that right after, she digs glasses out of her purse and puts them on.

The first thing I do is head for Lord & Taylor. Part

of my diet is eight glasses of water a day, which makes me a total pee-body. The department stores have the bathrooms.

I'm just washing my hands when my plan for peace and solitude gets blown up. Caroline Kennedy and Reenie Carrot barge in, their arms laden with shopping bags.

"Oh-mi-God. Sage!" Reenie squeals.

I used to hang with Reenie a lot, even though she's a rich girl. For one thing, her name is weirder than mine. For another, she likes *me*. She invites me to her parties and she belongs to the Thespians, although Madame Thespian never casts her in anything. Well, I liked Reenie until she talked me into running for class president.

Caroline's more of a foreign specimen. At every opportunity, she reminds you that, although she's not JFK's daughter, she has the same name, which means (she hints) she is somehow related to *the* Kennedys.

"I didn't know you shopped," Caroline says.

"It's a regular hobby of mine," I lie.

"We just got Halloween costumes," Reenie says.

I thought those were for kids. "Oh?"

"I'm going to be a bottle of ketchup."

"Wow."

"*Not.* I'm going as the Little Mermaid."

"I'm Cinderella," Caroline says. "We're all going as Disney Princesses. Mona's Belle, and Frida is Snow White."

"What are you going to be?" Reenie says.

Alone? "I usually just . . . hand out candy."

"No way!" Caroline says. "You've got to come to one of the parties. Bob Corney's is awesome. He makes this punch that has everyone so drunk, they're, like, *puking* within an hour."

"Sounds . . . fun."

"So Reenie, are you going to pee or what?"

Reenie goes into a stall.

"How long have you been here?" I ask Caroline.

"Just an hour. But I actually scored some good jeans. Gap is, like, the only company that understands my kind of butt." She turns to show me. "See, I have a bubble butt. Most jeans are for banjo butts. Let me see your butt."

Big fat butt, I think, but I turn to let her give me the verdict. "Your butt is kind of disappearing, Sage, if you want to know the truth."

"I had it when I left home," I joke.

"Seriously. Are you on a diet or something?"

"I guess it's a tennis racket butt." Answering that

question is like an admission of fatness. "There's holes in it."

"Help!" Reenie calls. "I don't have any toilet paper."

I grab some from another stall and drop it over the top. "You know who has a great butt." Reenie comes out. "Roger Willis."

"They're hot cross buns," Caroline says. "I'd like to take a bite out of them."

Which makes me pretty nauseous. "Well, see you guys," I say.

"Where are you going?"

"Uhhm." *Anyplace alone.* "Coach?"

"You need Coach," Caroline says. "Your purse is so . . ."

. . . *battered, from Target, sling bag, five bucks on sale two years ago.*

"Retro," Reenie says kindly.

"Yeah, you are so retro in your style, Sage. And roots are so in."

"If you just wait long enough, they come," I offer helpfully.

"We'll go with you," Reenie volunteers. "I love Coach."

"Great." I follow them to Coach, feeling both

annoyed and happy to be part of a group. The truth is, I'm not an insider, but I'm not an outsider, either, probably because at any occasion, I bring treats: the best fudge brownies, lemon bars, and cookies on the planet. Someday I'll write my own cookbook.

Inside Coach, Reenie starts draping purses on me.

"I can't wait to throw that thing in the trash." Caroline tugs on my purse.

"I'm attached to it." I tug back.

Most of the purses are locked in glass cabinets, but in the middle of the room there's a display of purses built into a pyramid.

"Look at that one at the top." Reenie points. "That's to die for."

So far, the purses have not tempted me . . . that much. Some are just plain plain; others have a pattern resembling the spermatozoa we studied in health. But this one is gorgeous, beige patterned with a zebra stripe down the middle, like my hair. My mouth actually waters.

"Go get the guy," Caroline orders.

Reenie dashes off and returns with the guy, who wields what looks like a giant fishing pole. "The Hamptons Zebra Stripe Satchel." He hooks it. "This is the last one. That's why I put it at the top."

"The last one!" Reenie swoons.

I try not to drool on it as I examine the price tag. *$368.00!*

"I don't like it," I say.

"But it's so you." Reenie is right: the size, the shape, the colors.

"Try it on!" Caroline demands. Still clutching my own piece of junk, I loop the work of art over my shoulder.

"It looks awesome with your new blonde hair with the roots showing."

I want it so much, but it is impossible!

This mom comes in with three kids, one about six, and the other two in a double stroller. She parks the stroller practically on top of us.

"Just take up the whole store, why doesn't she?" Caroline whispers.

"Watch Bim and Bip," the mom tells the six-year-old, and takes off.

"*Bim and Bip?*" Reenie mouths.

I take the momentary distraction to shed the purse.

"You have to buy it, Sage." Caroline picks it back up. "Doesn't she have to buy it?"

I don't know why she's so persistent!

"Definitely," Reenie says.

"I forgot my credit card," I offer lamely.

"No sweat," Reenie says. "You can use mine and just pay me back tomorrow."

$368; tomorrow?

"Oh-mi-God, he's picking his nose," Caroline says.

With one hand, Six is shoving the stroller back and forth in the aisle. With the other he is excavating his nose.

"Ewwww," Reenie says. "I hope he doesn't get boogers on the purses."

Nose-picker gives us a dirty look. Then, with a massive shove, he sends the stroller, toddlers and all, into the display. Caroline, leaning against the table, falls, the pyramid-o-purses tumbling on top of her.

It is a beautiful moment. Caroline Kennedy lying on the floor covered in thousands of dollars worth of Coach purses.

"What did you *do*?" The guy rushes toward us.

"Get me out of here!" Caroline shouts. Reenie and I each grab an arm and yank her up.

I give Nose-picker a big grin as we rush out the door into the cold free air.

I have got to get over my hostility toward other girls.

WAL-MART

Hypothetical question

IF YOU WERE A PICKLE, what kind would you be? Sweet or dill? Kosher? Would you come in slices? Or whole, soaking in briny fluid? Would you remain a cucumber? What if you were a sandwich? Would you be pastrami and Dijon on rye, or would you be the white-bread-and-mayonnaise type? Would you be the lunch meat: turkey? Bologna? Or one of those tomatoes that don't taste like anything, a manufactured tomato that has never seen the sun except through a glass ceiling, has never really lived at all?

SAGE

IF YOUR BODY were an object, what would it be? That was Bernstein's hypothetical question today. I wonder where he gets this stuff. Probably off the Internet; some teacher site like howtotortureyourstudents.com.

I actually like Bernstein's journal prompts. I keep up with them every day, unlike most kids, who write all of their entries at the end of the semester, then fudge the dates. A journal is something to trust, like an aunt you call for advice on makeup. Wish I had an aunt like that. Any relative would do. I would bake cookies for them. Mom must have a relative stashed away somewhere, an address in a drawer, a phone number, someone I could demand an explanation from: *Why is she like this?*

But I've just got the Goldburgs, a couple of once-in-a-while girlfriends, and this journal, my confessor.

Yesterday, at school, Reenie stole my journal entry.

"Sage!" She rushed up to me at my locker. "Bernstein is collecting our answers to the hypothetical questions today. Can you lend me yours? I have it next period and I'm desperate."

"Lend you?"

"Yeah. I never can think up anything original."

I opened up my notebook. The question was *If you were a country, which one would you be?* "We can't both have the same answer."

"I know. But you don't have English till fifth. You'll think up something else before then. You're brilliant at this stuff." She grabbed my notebook and ripped out the page. "I'll copy it over. Don't worry. He won't know the difference."

I was going to say no, but then I saw something that left me dumbfounded. The purse, my Coach Zebra purse, draped over her shoulder like no big deal.

"Thanks!" She was off before I could yank it off of her.

"But I wrote I was Sudan," I called after her. "Bernstein will never believe you're Sudan."

My journal and my purse; kind of like identity theft. Maybe that's why I had writer's block today. I looked at the question on the board and thought, *The blank page is a snowy mountain and I'm a downed skier.* But that wasn't the question.

If your body was an object . . .

Now, I can't stop thinking of answers. The body is an appliance, a map without borders. The body is a vessel of embarrassment: butt too big, hair too mousy (even highlighted), feet too wide. The body is a blob of Silly Putty, a whale, a bag of manure, a Dumpster, a floating barge. Only the hands are okay, long and thin, capable of kneading dough and decorating cakes. And maybe the legs. Yeah, the legs can hold their own.

x x x x

I would like to say I feel better. I would like to say that there are rewards for my efforts, which is what teachers and school counselors try to instill in you. But Mom's life dispels that myth. What is she if not one big failed effort? I wish I could stop thinking about her, feeling like she's my fault.

It's true that I am thinner by seven pounds. I can see that on the scale. It's just I still *feel* fat. I feel nothing like Mona, with her tiny waist and big green eyes, the way she walks through the hall and says hi to everyone, remembers their names and things about them—like they broke their elbow last summer, or they went to the Bruce Springsteen concert, or they love mangoes and she's brought them one.

When *I* walk through the halls at school, I keep my eyes on the floor, especially since that stupid election.

The only time I look up is when I hear Roger's big voice. My eyes are drawn to him like a paper clip to a magnet.

That's how I think of Roger. Big. Everything about him. His voice. His curls. His popularity. His muscles. His thick neck. A guy can be a barge. No problem. Then, if you're drowning, you can grab on to him. He would be unsinkable. He could save you.

VERN

YESTERDAY, Bernstein gave me a list of things to help with my writing notebook:

1.   Observe the details in life.

Okay. Here goes:

It is morning. Fall. Bright blue. No clouds. The cereal box is on the table. It is a kosher cereal because Sophie will only eat kosher. The cereal tastes like cardboard. The leftovers in Sophie's bowl (which she neglected to clear) look like a blob of barf. I stare out the window. There is a bird outside the window. On the telephone wire.

2.   Know the psychology of your characters.
The bird watches a squirrel below, then decides to scram in case the squirrel has bizarre, ulterior motives. At the moment it lifts off in flight, does the bird consider this a miracle?

I suck as a writer. I'm going to end up a lawyer, like Mom. My mind thinks like a lawyer, always weighing both sides of everything, looking for fairness.

Walter's the one who should write. I could never think up those hypothetical questions to torture my fellow students. And Sage. She's got voice. But Walter wants to be an architect and Sage wants to be a chef.

Last night, I took her to dinner at Thai Foon in Newport. After, we had a walk on the beach. The weather was perfect, just cold enough that she huddled close to me. I thought it was pretty romantic, but Sage only said the cold burned more calories. If she turns into one of these boring chicks who goes on about her weight, I'll freak! It's bad enough that she's made herself a blonde. And skinny. There's nothing left to hold on to.

Sage drove her mom's car because mine is in the shop having the snows put on. That car is scary. The defroster fogs the window. The windshield wipers shriek like some old lady shouting *Help!* at exact intervals. The tank said empty, but Sage wouldn't let me fill it. "You paid for dinner," she said, "and anyway, this thing lies."

Sage and her mom leave the key in the glove box, so after the lights went out at their house, I took the car to Exxon and filled up the tank.

Finally, because I couldn't sleep, I called Cassandra back. She'd left, like, six messages on my cell not to mention texting me constantly. Luckily, she didn't answer. Her message said, "Hi! I'm partying up a storm. I'll call you when I'm sober." Very classy.

SAGE

OUR FIRST THESPIANS MEETING. When Madame Thespian arrives, she'll announce the plays. It's always a Tennessee Williams, a holiday play, and a musical.

Everybody's here except Madame T., so I pass out the lemon bars I baked and the kids do monologues. Gary does "To be or not to be . . ." Lin Wong does Blanche DuBois. Reenie does Beth from *Crimes of the Heart*, only her Southern accent sounds like an English one.

What I like about theater is the same thing I like about cooking. You start with a few ingredients, and out of that, something amazing can come—although recipes are more dependable than actors.

Nobody says anything about my hair or weight loss. But I guess that's because I'm a behind-the-scenes kind of gal. Even in the career I want, as a chef, I will be invisible in the kitchen. Everyone does notice my lemon bars. Amber says they're heaven. Gary asks me to bring more next time.

"Let's give a hand to Sage," Lin says, "the best stage

manager on the planet!" and everyone claps, which feels kind of good, but embarrassing.

I wish there had been more of them so I would've had more votes.

I need to forget that stupid election.

Madame T. finally arrives, preceded by the smell of clove cigarettes and vodka. The fall play is *A Streetcar Named Desire*. Big surprise. The spring musical is *Grease*.

Barf. Why not *Les Miserables* or *West Side Story*? Now all the guys'll be doing their John Travolta imitations: "I got chills, they're multiplying . . ." I can't stand that song.

x x x x

After, I go out to the football field, hoping to run into Roger, but it's empty. He's probably in the locker room, so I wander through the parking lot looking for his car.

Roger drives a white pickup. The plate says: ROGERW. His parking space is 112. Just seeing that truck makes my heart pound.

No one's around, so I get up close. The truck's beat-up; the paint is scratched and the driver side door is wired shut. At least he's not a rich kid.

I peek in the window. There's a notebook on the

seat, some Snickers wrappers, fast-food bags, and crunched up Coke cans on the floor. Taped to the dashboard is a photo of Mona. That says it all.

x x x x

I don't even remember walking home; I was so upset and cold.

But now I'm here. Have you ever heard of a repetition compulsion? We're studying it in psych. It's doing the same thing over and over, even though it's destructive. I have that. Every day, when I come home, I expect to find a mom who gives comfort, or at least a bowl of soup. I wouldn't even mind if it was canned. But the house is dark. I can hear Mom in her room tearing things apart; paper ripping, like she's a hamster making a nest. She's got a rant going, but I don't listen. They're all the same, entertaining only for her.

There's no dinner, nothing in the fridge, and I can't find Selfish. Cramps hit me like a train wreck in my body.

I think about the white truck. And Mona. I've been wading in this little puddle of hope (or should I say, fantasy) for the last month and it's dried up. My stomach aches from hunger. The cramps cramp. Tears make their path down my cheeks. *What was I thinking?* Roger is going with Mona. I'll never be her. I should just feel lucky that I haven't been made fun of, the way Wal-Mart has all these years.

It takes me about ten minutes to find Selfish. He's sound asleep on a pile of laundry in the living room (Why is the laundry in the living room?).

I search for aspirin and tampons, but there's nothing, so I deal with a wad of toilet paper—pathetic—then head for my room.

On my bed is that book Mom keeps shoving at me: *The Purpose Driven Life*. The book is magic, Mom says. When some murderer in Atlanta broke into this lady's house, she showed him the book. He wept like a baby and let her go.

I tuck Selfish under the covers and get into bed next to him. Then I skim the first twenty pages. The book says that God decides your life. And God decides wisely. You just have to let go, to hand yourself over to God like you would to a beautician giving you a makeover.

"Okay, God," I say. "Take over. Send me a prince, a new dress. Change a pumpkin into Roger Willis." But that's not letting *Him* decide. "Just give me *something* to lift my spirits. Anything. I'm ready, God. Here's my life."

But I doubt that He hears. How could He with Mom

shrieking her prayers 24-7? Or with people starving and being wiped out by genocide, wars, and natural disasters?

God, if He exists, must have His hands fuller than full. Every day must be a bad day, and every night sleepless.

WAL-MART

Hypothetical question

IF YOU HAD TO CHOOSE a disability, which one would you have? Blindness? Down's syndrome? Cerebral Palsy? A missing limb? If you couldn't walk, would you be pushed around in a wheelchair, or would you build your upper body and race, never letting the obstacles in life stop you for a second?

SAGE

HALLOWEEN CAME AND WENT. I skipped the parties, since I didn't feel like making a lame costume, and carved a jack-o'-lantern, then sat by the door to give out candy. We only got ten kids. I could swear a bunch deliberately passed our house. Maybe they'd heard about the crazy woman who lives here.

The last to arrive were Vern and Sophie. Sophie was dressed as a Hasid, complete with those curls the Hasidic men wear—I forget what they're called.

"It's embarrassing. . . ." Vern teased her. "All these girls dressed as witches and fairies, and I get to cart around a religious extremist."

"Fundamentalist," Sophie corrected. She's an absolute genius.

"Same thing," Vern said.

"No. It's extreme based only on your perspective. Some people would say the way most Americans live is extreme: alcohol, drugs, mindless, empty sex, and all that other bad stuff."

"You're nine, Sophie. You're not supposed to talk about sex, mindless or otherwise." Vern shook his head.

"I calls 'em how I sees 'em."

"I think you look fantastic, Sophie," I told her. "I'll bet you have the most original costume."

"Well, I have to explain to everyone what my costume is and they get this sort of . . ."

"Stupefied," Vern suggested.

". . . yeah, stupefied look on their faces."

"What'll it be, sweetie?" I offered the bowl. "You can take all you want."

She turned into a kid then, and grabbed a handful of Almond Joys and peanut butter cups. "Thank you. Mom says it's okay not to be kosher for Halloween."

"Mom says it's okay not to be kosher at all."

"Vern?" I said, offering him the bowl.

"Anything homemade?"

"Didn't have time. Didn't have ingredients, either."

"Make a list. I'll get 'em for you."

I smiled. That's Vern. My whole life he's been right there, ready to give me anything I want.

The other notable thing about Halloween was Mom. She stayed out until two in the morning, never called me or anything. She could've borrowed someone's cell (hers met an untimely death when she threw it out the car window, combined with not paying her Verizon bill), or found a pay phone. I tried to go to bed, but I couldn't stop worrying.

When she finally stumbled in, she reeked of cigarettes. She must've been on a smoking spree. Her eye makeup was smudged. Her lipstick was all over her face.

"Where have you been?"

"Church. Where else?"

"Until two in the morning."

"I was talking to the reverend. He really is the most understanding man. And handsome!"

"Did you even think about calling me?"

"I didn't want to wake you. What were you doing?"

"Worrying!"

"We mustn't forget who the parent is here, Sage. It's my job to worry about you."

"No, we mustn't forget who the parent is!" I screamed, then I slammed into my room and locked the door.

For the rest of the night, she stood outside my door explaining how the reverend was leading her to God, and was probably in love with her, to boot.

Finally, I fell asleep, her crazy fantasies mixing with my worries, creating nightmares.

VERN

NEW IDEAS FOR A NOVEL: There's this disease going around, some kind of viral thing. It's because of the ozone layer. This guy who works in a tire store dreams the antidote to the disease. It's a combination of insect larvae, bee pollen, and foot fungus. At first everyone laughs at him. Greatness never comes easily. Finally, he succeeds and becomes famous. He falls in love with a girl who has light brown hair and big brown eyes. Only she has a crush on this total thug. Her name will be Page. She'll be smart, sweet, and totally without an ego. She'll make the world's best cookies and she'll cry loudly at the movies. The thug's name will be . . . Roger. Why not call a spade a spade. What's he gonna do? Sue me?

SAGE

WINTER WEATHER. The cold no longer nipping, but biting. The only time I'm warm is when I'm running. This morning I was going so fast I felt like sparks were flying off of my heels.

Thinness has its own energy. I never realized that before. I'd always thought it was food that gave energy.

Still, reading about that model who died of anorexia freaked me out. As not-so-great as my life has been, I'm kind of looking forward to the future, which I can, ideally, influence. I don't want to drop dead from starvation.

I need new clothes so badly. In addition to losing thirteen pounds, I seem to have grown an inch. My wrists are sticking out of the ends of my coat. There's less natural padding to keep me warm.

Last month, when I went to my orthodontist appointment, there was a newspaper clipping in the window saying that he had moved to India to work in a free clinic.

That's what Dr. Coner was like. He traveled to

Afghanistan and Iraq and had pamphlets in his office for a charity that gives goats and cows to poor people. He worked out a payment plan for my mom and was nice about the fact that she didn't pay it. "It all evens out," he said when I apologized. "Everything does. Trust me. It's the law of karma."

"What does that mean, exactly?" I'd asked him. "Karma."

"It means that the deeds you do and the choices you make will return to you in kind."

I liked that idea; cause and effect. "So if I'm nice and behave, good things will happen? Like that?"

"Uh-huh. And it carries over from one life to the next."

"Huh?"

"With each incarnation. So if you murdered someone in your last life, you'll spend this life paying the debt for it."

Karma carries over from *previous lives*? That took the fun right out of it.

Apparently, Dr. Coner had set out to earn some good karma, but who would tighten my braces? I wondered. Who would take them off at the end of the year? It's bad enough being the only senior with braces. I didn't want them for life!

Yesterday, though, I got a call from the new orthodontist.

"Hello, this is Coner Orthodontics. Is Mrs. Priestly there?"

Mom was locked in her bedroom in crash mode. "This is she," I lied.

"This is Dr. Pistachio. Your daughter, Sage, has an appointment this evening. I've just taken over the practice for Dr. Coner."

"Pistachio?"

"Please, no ice-cream cone jokes."

"No," I said. "I wouldn't."

"Of course not," he assured me. "Just every other character in town."

"What time is the appointment?" I asked, trying to sound old.

"Five thirty. The problem is . . . you'll have to enlighten me. The records are a bit of a mess. At what stage of the process is she?"

"At what stage?"

"Is this a tightening or a removal?"

I was about to say *tightening*. But then it came to me. The final step in my transformation. "Removal."

"Okay. Cool. Then we'll take some impressions for the retainer."

"Wonderful."

"You sound young," he said.

"I am. I had my daughter when I was fourteen."

I had to laugh at the silence on the other end.

✗ ✗ ✗ ✗

So I'm brace-less. My teeth look great, although they feel slimy and achy. The car had gas, miraculously. So now, I'm bopping through the market, buying groceries to make Mom a decent dinner.

She's flatlining again, which makes her more manageable, but more depressing, too. It's sort of my fault. Two nights ago, I came home from rehearsal to find some guy sitting on the couch, smoking a cigarette. He had gray hair in a mullet and wore a Harley T-shirt.

"Who are you?" I said, none too pleasantly.

"Jerry. I'm your mom's . . . well, I think I'm her date. She hasn't exactly said yet, but this feels like a date."

"When did you meet?"

"This afternoon. At AA. She spoke to the whole audience. She could make anyone sober. It was inspired."

"Alcoholics Anonymous?" Among my mom's many problems, drinking has never been one of them.

"Don't worry, I've been sober for three weeks."

to be Mona   **49**

"Where is she?"

"In the shower. Boy, she can talk. I've never met such a conversationalist. And smoke. She went through my whole pack."

It's an old trick of hers, bringing guys home. But she hasn't done it since she started going to church two years ago. It was like God became her boyfriend, a more dependable one. But something must've gone wrong with this reverend, because she hasn't talked about him in days; now this.

"I think it's time for you to go. My dad will be home in about five minutes, and he is big and very angry."

"You're shitting me. She said her husband was a 'no-show.'"

"Oh, he's a 'show,' all right. And my dad told me if my mom brings men home to call the police." I went to the phone. "He put the last guy in the hospital. Nine-one-one . . ." I started to dial.

"I'm going. I don't need any trouble. I was just trying to have a good time. I was gonna take her for dinner." He stopped at the door. "Truth be told, you're kind of a bitch."

A compliment, under the circumstances. "Out!"

Mom sobbed and screamed like a two-year-old

when she came out and found him gone. "You sent my boyfriend away! Out of sheer jealousy."

"Yeah. Right. I've always had a thing for toothless alcoholics."

When she was done with the drama, she took to bed, where she's been ever since. And yeah, I did feel kind of guilty spoiling her fun, which is why I'm at the market now getting groceries to make her a nice dinner.

"Ms. Priestly." It's the store manager. He's a short, pudgy man with red hair and a gray mustache. He's asked my mom out on dates six or seven times, and I wouldn't have minded her going out with *him*, but of course she said he was too boring. "Hi, Mr. Murphy."

"H-hello. How is your mother? Well, I hope?"

"The usual."

"I-I'm afraid there's something a little difficult."

"What?"

"Your mom's line of credit. The bill . . ." He leans in. "It hasn't been paid since August."

I look in my cart: my post-braces snacks, the dinner ingredients, coffee, toilet paper (which we are almost out of), cat food, sugar, eggs, milk, Tampax. Blood rises to my face.

Mr. Murphy's face is also red. "She used to pay the first of every month like . . . clockwork, so I've tried to let it go. But just yesterday, I got a very heated letter from the company. Businesses just aren't the way they used to be. They're so . . . corporate."

I want so badly to run out the door. "I'm so sorry. I didn't know . . ."

"Do you have cash with you today?"

Like a lame-o, I pull a quarter out of my pocket. My eyes fill and I wish for an earthquake to open a crack in the floor and suck me in.

"Tell you what. We'll just take out a couple of items, and send you through, but I won't be able to extend credit after today. It's just not possible."

"Of course not."

"I'll just . . ." He pulls out the goat cheese and the coffee, plus chocolate chips. He looks even more embarrassed when he sees the Tampax and toilet paper. "That'll do," he says. "Take the rest."

"Thank you," I gasp. "I'm sorry."

He pulls my cart forward and nods to the checkout girl. She gives me a dirty look, but puts my groceries through.

Once I'm out the door, I take a quick look back and

see Mr. Murphy pulling money out of his own wallet and handing it to her.

X X X X

You wonder how much worse things can get, and the answer is . . . a lot.

I must have been awful in my past life.

WAL-MART

Hypothetical question

IF YOU WERE A WEB SITE, which one would you be? What if you were a dictator, a criminal, a war, a body odor: halitosis or a fart?

✗ ✗ ✗ ✗

I'm sick of coming up with these questions for Bernstein. How did I end up with this? Oh yeah, he let me out of the final exam last year during my little bout of suicidal depression. This is both reparation and therapy.

Bernstein has a good heart. He favors the underdogs; probably was one himself.

Senior year. Got to keep up the grades and get into a good school, then everything will be peachy. Strive. Strive. Make a life with some swell guy, a Soho loft, a Victorian in San Fran, where it's normal to be ten steps left of center.

Too much caffeine today. That's why I can't sleep. My brain's on overload, missiles flying, sparks igniting, particles shifting, synapses synapsing.

Vern and I have been such café junkies lately. We've analyzed it as escape from the moms and their tragic expressions—*Our babies are leaving home!*

When I can't sleep, like this, I design buildings in my head: a tree house loft, a mountain dwelling, an underwater oasis, an abode hung from skyhooks that seems to float in space. The benefits of such a nest are obvious. You are above it all. Head in the clouds, a reality.

The furniture would have to be as light as bird skeletons. The beds, feather. The plumbing, guided by gravity. If someone you didn't like walked underneath your house, someone who'd tormented you, like the entire football team, you could just flush the toilet and let the sewage drop on their heads.

SAGE

ALMOST THANKSGIVING. It's hard to believe. The giant stuffed turkey mascot with the wobbly head is perched atop the trophy case. It is one scary bird.

"Sage!" Reenie rushes up to me.

"I don't have any extra journal entries," I say.

"Oh." She winces. "I meant to tell you. Bernstein was kind of pissed that I used your entry. He is so sketchy."

"He found out?"

"He could tell it was yours from the writing style."

"Great."

"Plus, he didn't believe that I would compare myself to Sudan. Miami Beach or Beverly Hills, maybe. Don't be mad, okay? You know I think you're so cool. You're such a good writer and cook. You're not afraid to be yourself."

Which feels like an insult somehow.

"Here. Have a double mocha latte. I bought it for Mona, but I can't find her to save my life."

Getting Mona's latte seems like a good sign, like opening a fortune cookie and being told you're headed for greatness. I am so caffeine starved.

The sound of wind chimes comes from her phone. She digs in *my* purse for her cell. "Hi, Daddy." She waves to me and dashes off.

Daddy. That word. To this day, it gives me a hollow feeling where the food goes. I should get over it.

I slink into history late, but it doesn't matter. Mr. Jess isn't there yet. Every day, he's thirty seconds later. By January, he might just stop coming altogether.

Kids are going on about the hypothetical questions, which are getting weirder. Last week's was *If you had to donate an organ, which one would it be?* Rumor is they're written by a student.

"If I find the little bastard who's coming up with this stuff," Al Smith says, "I'll clobber him." Al Smith is all muscle, even between his ears. He's on the football, wrestling, and soccer teams. Baseball would be too civilized for him.

"What makes you think it's a guy?" Candid Craver says.

"If you were a sex act," Fern Weaver jokes, "which one would you be?" Fern moved here this year from California and became one of the popular girls right away, although she's not identified with any one group.

Jess comes in, looking totally miserable. Maybe it's

thinking about history all the time, the horrible things humans have done to each other. "Whoever has cappuccino, get rid of it. It's making me jealous."

I hide it under the desk.

"The ten of you who are text messaging can put away your phones."

No one moves.

"Now!" A bunch of kids put their phones away.

Jess launches into a speech about the Nazis and the concentration camps. Which makes me nauseous. Every time he goes on about Jews being exterminated, I picture the Goldburgs. I mean, the Goldburgs are the greatest people. Vern's mom is a public defender and volunteers for a million things. His dad is a social worker and coach. Sophie is a genius. Then there's Vern: top student, funny as hell, and nice as heaven.

Al Smith raises his hand. "My dad says the Holocaust is fiction. It's like this huge conspiracy, a cover-up, to justify the Israeli treatment of the Palestinians."

"Yeah," Vicky Shelby adds. "It's like in that old movie *Wag the Dog*."

This is what happens when you're not in honors classes. You get all of the morons. Now, if I actually had done my homework the last three years, I could be in with Vern and Wal-Mart, and yeah, Mona.

Mr. Jess snatches a folder off his desk and pulls out photographs. "I was going to spare you the evidence. . . ." He passes around Holocaust photographs: pits filled with dead bodies, skeletons standing at the gates of a concentration camp.

"Here's another photograph." He pulls out his wallet. "These are my grandparents: Sara and Jacob Hillman. It was said that they died at Bergen-Belsen, but maybe it was just a fantasy. They never existed at all. And I'm a ghost in front of you."

The class gets totally quiet.

"Tell you what." Mr. Jess's voice is shaky. "The first stop on our senior trip to DC will be the Holocaust Museum. That might convince at least some of you to pay attention to history."

A few kids groan. The bell rings. I lag behind to, I don't know, offer support to poor Mr. Jess, who is raking his hands over his nonexistent hair. "Mr. Jess?"

"Yes, Sage."

I want to say I'm sorry about the idiots in this class, sorry about his grandparents, but all I can muster is: "I'm sorry I can't go on that spring trip. It sounds really interesting."

"I'm sorry too. You're one of the few sane people in this class."

I feel myself blush, because, even if it is from Mr. Jess, compliments are hard to come by. And being called sane. Wow. That's a treat when you have a mom like mine. "Well . . . on to lunch."

He smiles. "Next time, bring me some coffee too."

✗ ✗ ✗ ✗

The first person I see in the lunch room is Mona. She's wearing a gorgeous leather jacket, and the most beautiful pink suede boots I have ever seen. Her hair is piled up on her head, tousled but perfect.

Mona looks like she's going to speak to me in that phony sweet way. Luckily, Vern is waving like a madman, as if I haven't sat with him for lunch every school day of my life. I turn my back on her and head for him.

"What's with the getup?" Vern says.

"What?"

"You've been wearing black for, like, ten years. Now, for the third day, colors."

"I'm reinventing myself."

"Why? I love you just how you are."

"No one stays how they are, Vern. Not even you." He does look really different; grown-up. He's gained weight and bulked up. "You look good. Are those new glasses?"

"They were new two months ago! So what are you and your mom doing for Thanksgiving?"

"I don't know yet."

"You guys are invited to our house."

"Cool."

"My mom went over to ask your mom, but she said your mom was kind of . . . unresponsive."

"She's lucky she wasn't in one of her 'responsive' moods. Those are a lot worse."

"Yeah. I wish . . ."

"What?"

"I wish she was better," he says softly.

"We'll come. Thanks."

"Do you have to do the big history paper? I think it really sucks to assign a ten-page research project to seniors. Like we don't have enough to do applying to colleges."

"We only have to do five pages. I still don't have a topic. What are you doing yours on?"

"The relationship between civility and barbarism, like how the Germans were so cultured, but then became Nazis."

"Good topic."

"Walter thought it up."

"Maybe I should talk to him about my paper."

"You should talk to Walter, just to, you know, talk to him."

"Yeah, it's just . . ."

"What?"

"He's on such a different wavelength from anyone else. I said hi to him the other day and he jumped, like, three feet."

"Maybe he has a crush on you."

"Isn't he gay?"

"Okay, maybe it's *me* who has a crush on you."

I slug him. "Cut it out. You're like my brother."

"In certain ancient cultures, brothers and sisters did marry each other in order to preserve the pure lines of ancestry."

"Stop."

"Okay. But this is your last chance. You can have me, who loves you for who you are, or the big dumb tank who could never even *see* you for who you are." He gestures toward Roger, who is devouring a cheeseburger at the jock table.

"I don't think *having him* is one of my options."

"You never know."

"Why did you say it's my last chance?"

Cassie Parks, who has effective blonde highlights and a manufactured tan plops down next to Vern.

"Wow, Vernie, can you believe I *just* got done with my home yech test. I had to stay after the bell rang."

"What was it on?"

"Measurements, you know, like for recipes. Only Mrs. Farley would turn cooking into math. She's such a skank. You can see why her husband dumped her for Ms. Green. So . . ." She leans against his shoulder. "Did you decide about whether you're going to homecoming with me? You said you'd give me an answer."

"Uh . . ." Vern slides a look at me. I stick my tongue out at him; we've gone to just about every dance together since middle school.

"Oh, hey Sage, I didn't notice you," she says.

"Hey, Cassie," I say, trying to sound sweet, coming out sour.

"I'm going by Cassandra now. You know, like that psychic chick from Greek mythology, as opposed to that little pink character from *Dragon Tales*."

"The mythical Cassandra was cursed," Vern informs her. "She could see the future, but no one believed her."

"Really, Vernie? That is so sad."

"He's going by *Vern* now," I say.

"I'll go with you, Cassandra," Vern says.

"Cool, because I already posted it on MySpace that

we were going together. My dad'll pay for a limo. It will be so rad. I've picked out my dress. It's salmon, so try to get a matching tie. Well, I gotta go. I told Mona and them that I'd join them for lunch. Nice shirt, Sage. Where'd you get it? Salvation Army?"

"Nordstrom."

"Yeah. Right." She teeters away on her high heels.

"Vernie." I make a barfing gesture.

"I gave you last chance."

"Yeah, thanks. You didn't say anything about the homecoming dance."

"I want to go, just this once, with someone who'll actually kiss me. With their mouth open!"

"Jerk."

"Thanks. You do look pretty in that color."

"I got it at Salvation Army," I admit.

"You're not mad at me?"

"It's on MySpace already. How can I be mad?" I say, feeling furious.

"I was hoping you'd be jealous, at least."

"I'm not jealous," I lie. "I'm just . . ."

"What?"

"Nauseous."

"That makes two of us." He points.

Roger Willis and Al Smith are arm wrestling at their

table, cheered on by the other football players.

"Watch this!" I grab a lunch tray from the table and make my way through the crowd. The photo of Mona taped to Roger's dashboard blinks on and off in my mind like a war scene you can't forget. *Last chance.*

I use my tray to slice through the bodies, get right up next to Roger, and drop it crashing to the floor. *LOOK AT ME!*

Everything goes quiet. Roger drops Al's arm, reaches down for the tray, his eyes moving up my legs, my body, then fixing on my face. He holds it out to me. I try to take it back, but he doesn't let go of it. He just stares at me and holds it (holds me) until I start to giggle.

"Nice smile," he says.

ROGER

"SAY YOUR MIND IS A ROOM," Bernstein goes in English today. "What are the furnishings?"

Mona starts writing immediately, Miss *full of ideas*, Miss *I just don't want to go out with you, Roger. Sorry. It's never going to happen.* Like she couldn't have told me that freshman year, and saved me the trouble of asking her out forty-six times over four years. I have counted them.

Come to think of it, I don't remember her going out with anyone. Yeah, she'll go to a dance with some guy, get crowned. She'll hug the football player who made the winning touchdown. But that's it. For all I know, she could be a lesbo. I should fix her up with Wal-Mart. But then again, *not*. A lesbo wants another lesbo, not a faggot.

That new girl wasn't bad. The one who dropped her tray. She wasn't *the kind*, but there was something in her eyes, deerlike, that got to me, the way she tugged that tray like she was asking me for a favor. Her smile was sweet. And her legs were amazing. I asked George and Randy about her and they said, "What new girl?"

So I still don't know who she is. I'll look for her again at lunch tomorrow.

Say your mind is a room . . .

Journaling sucks. Big time.

. . . a room.

I need to transfer out of this class.

Last night on *COPS* there was a car chase. The criminal dude jumps out of the car in this residential neighborhood and the cops chase him into people's yards. Even the cameraman is running. You can hear him panting; he's out of shape. The criminal jumps over a wall and the cops are freaked, but then one gets up in a tree, and he jumps on the dude and knocks him down. The cop breaks his femur. But the criminal is on his face in handcuffs.

x x x x

That's what I'm after. The real world. Life as it happens. Not this fake crap. All these girls like Mona with their college applications and *life goals* burn me up. It's like some hag feminist told them that what they should expect in life is everything, but without lifting a finger.

One day, when I'm a cop, I'll pull Mona over and give her a ticket. I won't give her a break. Maybe I'll even find a way to arrest her. Probable cause.

That's the room I see in my brain: a jail cell. The furnishings are some cots, a sink, a broken toilet, and a cement floor. And criminals; yeah, the scum of the earth, one by one, filling up that cell. Me bringing them in handcuffed, giving the losers a tour of their nice new surroundings.

SAGE

I'VE LIVED HAPPILY FOR A WEEK on *nice smile*, but its luster is wearing off. I feel like Cinderella after midnight, when her coach turned into a rotting pumpkin and the drivers into rats. I've also gained back two pounds.

To thank Vern for agreeing to take Cassie to the dance, I sat with Caroline, Fern, and Reenie at lunch. Reenie's migrated toward Fern's group since Madame T. once again did not cast her in the Christmas play. I don't know; if I was a high school drama teacher, I would make sure everyone got to be in a play, not just pick favorites.

After two days of being ignored, Vern cornered me. "What's the matter, Sage? We're not friends anymore?"

The look on his face made my stomach flip-flop, like when I see Roger. "I'm punishing you because you're not taking me to the dance."

"Don't punish me. I'll take you."

I felt like a rat. Vern is cute, smart, and funny. He deserves a girlfriend. "It's okay."

"I was just being immature."

"The dance is tomorrow night and she's hired a limo."

"I guess." He looked miserable. "Are you going to go? We could at least dance together."

"Nah. But it means a lot that you were willing to dump her." I kissed his cheek.

"So you'll sit with me today?"

"Of course. You're my best friend."

"Thanks," he said, but he didn't look too happy.

x x x x

The day got a bit better after that, although no prince appeared. Gary cornered me at rehearsal and asked me to help him practice his lines. Ben Sterum, this good-looking preppy kid, grabbed my books and carried them into history. Even Wal-Mart waved at me in the hall. He moved his hand up and down like a karate chop. I think it was a wave. Then, when I was dressing for PE, Fern Weaver came over. "How mortified were you the other day?"

I scanned my brain for an episode of embarrassment. Did I trip or spill milk on myself? Or was I just being me?

"We are in class with a bunch of Nazis," she added. "I felt so sorry for Mr. Jess."

"Oh, yeah. That was awful."

"So, what are you doing after school? Brad scored some stuff and we're going to Newport to hang out."

Stuff? It took me a minute to figure out she meant drugs. "I'm going to the movies with Vern."

"Vern? Are you guys merged?"

"Merged?"

"Like married? You're always together."

"Nah. We're just friends. He lives next door to me."

"I guess that scares away the guys."

"Huh?"

"Everyone thinks you're an item."

"Really?" Does Roger? Maybe that's why no one ever asks me out.

"If you change your mind, text me."

"Okay."

"You want to put my number in your cell?"

Yeah. Right. "It's not on me. Just write it down."

"The old-fashioned way." Fern dug a receipt out of her purse and wrote down her number. "Some day, we're not even going to learn to write. They'll just teach kids to type. Ta."

After she left, I turned over the receipt. It was for Applebee's. Sixty-five dollars. It must be nice.

x x x x

The last period of the day, I got even more attention, but it wasn't of a great kind. Bernstein asked me to stay after class.

"Ever thought of being a writer?" he asked, which threw me.

"I want to be a chef."

"Why is it that the students who are the best writers aren't the ones who want to *be* writers. And the ones who desperately want to write don't have the talent."

Yikes. I hope he's not talking about Vern. "Words are like ingredients in a recipe. I like to play with them and create a new dish."

"See what I mean," he went. "You've got originality. So when your writing shows up in another student's hands, it's quite obvious."

I held my breath. "Sorry."

"Reenie said she just 'borrowed' it from you. . . . She didn't ask."

Thank you, Reenie!

"Yeah, kind of."

"Don't let it happen again."

"I won't."

"Stand up for yourself. Okay? I know it's not your habit, but you're going to have to learn."

It's not my habit? *How does he know that?* "I'll try."

"I've sent a note to the guidance department. I want you moved to A.P. English next semester."

✗ ✗ ✗ ✗

When I get home, Mom is in bed with the lights out. As much as I hate her crazy periods where she's all hyper and revved up, this is worse, like living with a corpse.

"I'm getting transferred to A.P. English," I announce to her door.

"Come in," she moans. "Don't turn on the light."

"I got into A.P. English." I go into the scary, dark dungeon.

"I used to love English. Do you remember how I wrote poems for you when you were little? I would read them to you while you were eating your Cheerios."

As usual, it's all about her. "I don't remember."

"You had such a sweet face and big round eyes like chocolate cakes. When you went to preschool, I would cry. I missed you so much; I cleaned the house until it shined." Her voice turns sour. "Then Robert would come home with his muddy shoes and walk through the kitchen."

"Guess you don't have that problem anymore," I say.

"You used to be so nice," she says. "When you were little, I thought, *I should've named her Sugar. There's no wisdom there, but is she ever sweet.* So be sweet. For once."

"Why don't you get out of bed."

"I can't. I'm sick. I want to die."

"You'll feel better if you get up and turn on the lights."

"I have a headache the size of . . ." Her voice is dull. ". . . the size of something large. Get me an aspirin."

"There's no aspirin. I had cramps the other day and I couldn't find any."

"Go to the store."

"Vern's taking me to the movies."

"You need to take care of *me*! There's three dollars in my purse. I won't live through the night without aspirin."

It's eighteen degrees outside. The car door is frozen shut. I yank so hard the door flings open and I slip on the ice, landing on my hip. Now my jeans are torn. And my hand is scraped. I guess two of us need aspirin.

The tank is on empty again. *Where does she go?* I drive to Brooks on a prayer.

There's about a hundred different kinds of aspirin. I scan the prices until I find the cheapest.

"Hey."

My heart stops; I am so tuned in to that voice.

"How's it going?"

Roger is wearing a black turtleneck. His cheeks are redder than usual. He looks gorgeous.

"Hi." It comes out squeaky.

"You're the new girl," he says.

"Me?"

"Yeah. You dropped your tray the other day. Remember? I picked it up for you."

"Right. Thanks."

"You don't remember?"

"Uhhm."

"Everyone's nervous when they're new. What's your name?"

"Sage."

"Pretty name. I'm Roger."

"I know."

"I think there's another Sage at our school."

I don't want to tell him that I'm that "other Sage." But I can't really lie. I give my best Mona smile, the *This-is-the-Miss-America-Contest-and-I-am-going-to-work-with-disabled-children* smile. "I'm not really new."

"I would've noticed you before."

My tongue swells like I have a shellfish allergy and have just eaten shrimp. Could I be drooling? "Nope. I'm old," I try to joke.

"You're new to me, and you're news to me."

"Good news, I hope." Which would be okay, if it didn't come out in the world's dorkiest voice.

"You've got great eyes. You know what they remind me of? Deer eyes. A doe's."

"Uh, well . . ." I hold up the aspirin. "Gotta get this aspirin to my mom. She's got a headache the size of Texas." *Now, how did that pop into my brain?*

"I'll see you soon." He says it like a promise.

I try not to limp as I walk away. Idiot! I'm right there with him and I end the conversation.

The whole drive home I go over the conversation: *Great eyes. Doe eyes.* That means he likes my eyes. Maybe he even thinks I'm pretty.

I got chills, they're multiplying. . . .

WAL-MART

Multiple Choice

A GUY IS GAY BECAUSE:

1. When he was little his mom wore red lipstick too often. She bought him clothes that were too small. When she cleaned, she wore yellow latex gloves that gave him nightmares about certain foreign objects: gift boxes, radios, and trains. She cleaned too much. The house was too messy. She yelled at him. She was too quiet. She was afraid of flying. (I.e., everything is the fault of the mother.)

2. His uncle molested him in the swimming pool when he was six. Or four. Okay, not the swimming pool, and not the uncle. A neighbor with a penchant for raking leaves and fondling boys. Nobody molested him. He saw the giraffes at the zoo and had a transformation. He wore pink diapers. He had a ruffled quilt. Ruffles. Pink. Need I say more.

3. It was the priest's fault.

4. None of the above. He was born that way.
5. It's just a stage.

x x x x

I've had a lot of *stages*. I had the Pokémon stage, the SimCity stage, the anime stage, the Nintendo DS stage, the solitary confinement stage. My favorite was the agoraphobia stage, where I wouldn't leave the house. I missed a whole year of school for that one.

I had the amphetamine stage, my life fragmented like I had razor blades in my brain, the alcohol stage, the suicidal stage, the death-poetry stage, the stand-up comedian stage, only I wasn't funny.

Being gay is not a stage.

x x x x

My latest shrink says, "You're self-destructive." And I listen because my mom looked so desperate when she brought me here. It makes me feel like I'm a pack mule climbing up some difficult trail. Carrying her expectations and dashed hopes on my back.

The shrink before this one used to fall asleep. He would glaze over and I could say anything. I'd recite physics equations or explore fractals. He would nod.

"You're self-destructive," New Shrink says. I thought they were supposed to pose questions.

Moi? Because I tried to hang myself last year? Nah.
"Am I?" I pose a question.

"Yeah."

"Better than destructive to others, don't you think? There's too much of that going around. Like terrorists who destroy themselves and take out others with them, in the name of God."

"What are you saying?" N.S. leans forward.

"Like suicide bombers."

"Are you planning . . . to take out others?"

From his Psychology 101 class. It's chilling to be asked such a question. Like I have ever hurt anyone. "I just said I wasn't. Didn't I?"

"I just want to be sure."

The guy has degrees on the wall, a row of squares reflecting light against the wall. Boxes. Boxes.

You've made up your mind about me, New Shrink, and it has nothing to do with me. "Be sure," I go.

"You mentioned God."

"Yeah?"

"Do you believe in God?"

"My God is Franz Kafka."

"Who is that? Is it a cult?"

He doesn't know who Kafka is! "Jewish. A writer. He died of TB." Now he is totally written off.

"That's too bad."

"It was lucky."

"What do you mean by that?" He leans forward.

"The rest of his family died in concentration camps."
Why am I bothering?

"So what is it about this . . . writer that seems important to you?"

"He presented reality."

"As?"

"Absurd."

"Give me an example."

I'm too well brought up to sigh as loudly as I want to. "Like in *The Trial* a man is arrested for a crime he didn't commit, then he believes he's guilty. In *The Castle* a land surveyor searches for the castle, but can never reach it."

"Sounds like he writes about madness." Very pleased with himself.

"But he's not the mad one. It's society. The machine."

Deep sigh. "Your mother tells me that you've recently quit all extracurricular activities."

"My only activity was making up assignments for some teacher. Journal prompts. I was sick of doing it."

"Does that seem healthy? Quitting an extracurricular activity in the middle of senior year? Aren't you worried about getting into college?"

"I have straight A's and an almost perfect score on the SATs. I assume I'll get in *somewhere*."

The shrink wipes his hand across his forehead. "Let's talk about your sexual orientation."

Another box. I look out that square window, like a TV screen on the wall. A single tree limb is there, one dead leaf dangling from it, the last one. And even though it's a windy day, the leaf is holding on. Scared shitless of falling.

SAGE

HAPPY THANKSGIVING. Selfish and I are baking a pie and catching up on homework.

Bernstein said no more hypothetical questions. The class applauded, but I was disappointed. I enjoy them, as crazy as they are.

Instead, we had to make a list of things we're thankful for. That's almost as good as writing about your summer vacation.

My list: I am thankful that . . .

1. I do not live in a mud village in India.
2. I do not have AIDS.
3. Even though Selfish is thirteen, he still seems healthy.
4. We were invited to the Goldburgs so that Thanksgiving will not be a total wreck, and I have given myself permission to eat all I want. (Besides, I read that feasting occasionally speeds up your metabolism, thus enabling you to get more out of dieting.)

I didn't write that I was thankful for *nice smile* and *great eyes*, because that's private. I didn't write that sometimes when I look in the mirror, I think, *not bad.*

✗ ✗ ✗ ✗

With the money I made from raking leaves, I bought baking ingredients, coffee, a carton of cigarettes for Mom, and a ball of yarn for Selfish. He's a bit confused about its purpose, though. He keeps sitting on it, like it's an egg.

I check the pie. It looks incredible. The secret is to whip the eggs until they're practically meringue and to make the pumpkin smooth. The butter for the crust has to be really cold when you start.

I pour a mug of coffee for Mom. I can't remember when she last left the bed.

There was a time when I enjoyed her mood swings, at least the highs. We would stay up all night and watch old movies. Or we would drive to the beach and look at stars through the telescope. Once, when she got fired from the A&P, we toilet papered the store manager's house in the middle of the night.

But the next day I'd have to go to school and I'd be exhausted, while Mom would go back to bed.

I guess my attitude changed when I started to *care* what my future might be, to consider what other people thought of us, to wish there were groceries in the fridge. I started feeling embarrassed by the piles of laundry, the greasy carpet, the cigarette butts on the floor and the burns on the coffee table, the way she would corner people and talk, while they told her they were in a rush and had to go.

Things are getting so much worse. I don't know what to do. The electric bill is due. I wonder if she's paid the mortgage. She promised to go to social services and apply for aid, but that would mean getting out of bed.

It's embarrassing. The kids at school who have new cars, laptops, cell phones, and designer clothes don't have a clue what my life is like, thank God. They think I dress the way I do because I'm eccentric, a theater geek. What was it Reenie called me? *Retro.* No one around here can imagine anybody poor.

I put in applications at CVS, Cumberland Farms, Job Lot, Bread and Comfort, Starbucks, and about ten other places. That's the only solution to the immediate problem: get a job.

x x x x

I go in Mom's room and open the blinds. "Happy Thanksgiving."

Mom covers her eyes. "Close those."

"God, Mom. This room is a mess."

"Who cares?"

I hand her the coffee and prop up her pillows. She sips it like an invalid. "It's noon, Mom. We're supposed to be at the Goldburgs' at one, so you'd better shower."

"I can't be around people right now."

"For once, don't disappoint me."

"You can go without me. You love those people. You think they're God's gift. Besides, I hate turkey. Their feet look like the claws of wicked old ladies. They have these jowls like the chins of old men."

"That's how they look when they're alive!"

"Then they put the stuffing in that place, the cavity. Why is it called that? Like something you get in your tooth. Normally, with meat, they disguise the names, so you don't know what you're eating. Like pork or steak. Turkey, they call turkey. There's no disguising that."

It's starting. The transition from zombie to madwoman. It always begins like this, with her saying eccentric things that will get crazier as the week goes on.

"Look. All you have to do is eat and not say much. Right? Especially the 'not say much' part."

"Miriam Goldburg used to be my friend."

"She's still your friend. That's why you were invited."

"We strolled you and Vern together. We got hot fudge sundaes. Later, Miriam would only eat fruit or have a Diet Coke. That was annoying. She's always been slightly overweight with a big butt. Do you remember?"

"Right, I remember everything about being one."

"What's that smell?"

"Pumpkin pie."

"It smells like screeching tires."

"Okay, you win. I'll just go for an hour. I'll tell them you don't feel well, then I'll bring you home a plate of food."

"I'm going." She swings her legs off the bed. "You're not spending a holiday without me. I'm your mother."

"Please." I grab her arm. "Just behave normally."

"Don't I always?"

✗ ✗ ✗ ✗

Sophie greets us at the door. "Happy Thanksgiving."

"Hello, beautiful," I say.

"I'm not beautiful. People keep saying I look like Anne Frank, like that's a cheerful thing. Did Vern tell you I started Yeshiva last week? Now I truly feel like I belong."

"So you're not going to Goddard any more?"

"The kids made fun of me there, because I said prayers before I ate and was kosher and stuff like that. Mom didn't want me to go to Yeshiva. She says I'm too obsessed with religion."

"You can never be too obsessed with God," Mom says.

"I agree," Sophie says. "That's a nice dress, Mrs. Priestly."

"I used to have a pink dress but I can't find it."

Vern and Mr. and Mrs. G. descend, shower us with hugs, tug us into the warm house, and hand out drinks. The table is set with a gold tablecloth, pumpkin-colored napkins, and a centerpiece made of acorns, pinecones, and ribbons. The china is black with gold trim. It's like walking into *Martha Stewart Living*. "This is so beautiful."

"Not as beautiful as your pie," Mrs. G. says.

"I'm salivating." Vern loves my baking.

X X X X

Before dinner, Sophie says a prayer. I always love the Hebrew prayers. Maybe it's because I don't understand the words.

"I'd like to add a prayer," Mom says loudly.

"By all means," Mr. G. says.

"Hail Mary, full of Grace," Mom begins. "The Lord is with thee. Blessed art thou amongst women, and blessed is the fruit of thy womb, Jesus. Jesus is our Lord and our God—"

"That's good, Mom," I interrupt.

"Very nice," Mr. G. says. "What a nice prayer."

"Thank you." Mom beams. "I'm not really a Catholic anymore, but that was our Catholic prayer when I was little."

"Oh?" Mrs. G. says. "What are you?"

"Just a straight Christian, Miriam. Nothing between me and God."

x x x x

Dinner goes pretty well for the first fifteen minutes, probably because everyone is so busy eating.

Mr. G. and Vern chat about football. Sophie shares her plan to become a rabbi. Mrs. G. talks about being a public defender. "When I was on my own, I had the most trivial cases: a couple who wanted to redefine their property lines, personal injury suits that amounted to me settling with insurance companies, a man who got a chicken bone stuck in the side of his mouth and wanted to sue the restaurant . . ."

"She won him a six-hundred-thousand-dollar settlement and he didn't even have to go to the doctor," Mr. G. brags.

"Now I'm representing a homeless man who was beaten by the police, a woman who ran over her husband after she caught him cheating, and this man who went into a nursing home and started shooting."

"This is really cheerful stuff for Thanksgiving, Mom," Vern chides.

"Five people saw him do it. The physical evidence is insurmountable. But the guy thinks I'm the enemy for trying to get him to make a plea bargain."

"You know who the real enemy is. . . ," Mom offers.

"Who?" Mrs. G. asks.

"Gravity."

Everyone laughs, and I silently pray that this is as wacky as she gets.

"I'm not kidding," Mom says. "You look in the mirror and everything is drooping."

"More wine, Eve?" Mr. G. offers.

"Why, yes, thank you, Peter. You're a lovely host."

"Thank you."

"It's been so long since we socialized that I forgot just how wonderful you are." Mom stares at him.

"Can you believe our kids are graduating this year, Eve?" Mrs. G. says. "I remember when they used to run around the yard for hours, playing imaginary games."

"And Vern used to get himself all in a tangle," Mom says. "Wasn't that funny? He'd just fall and his arms and legs would be every which way."

"No," Mrs. G. corrects. "He did that on purpose. He didn't fall. He was just phenomenally limber."

"I wanted to be an acrobat in the circus," Vern says.

"Those days are gone," Mrs. G. says. "Now all we think about are college applications. Vern's been working on his essay for two months! I read an article somewhere that said that fifty percent of college applicants do not write their own essay. Can you believe that? Fifty percent."

"I read an article about teens," Mom says. "It's about *rainbow parties*. Do you know what that is?"

Vern's eyes go wide.

"Mom!" I warn.

"It's where a bunch of girls wear different colored lipstick and then they go in the bedroom with a boy and—"

"Eve!" Mrs. G. nods toward Sophie. "Can we please not talk about that right now?"

"Of course, Miriam. You always have liked to be in control of the conversation."

"Where are you applying, Sage?" Mr. G. asks.

"Uhm, I don't know."

"Mrs. Priestly," Vern says. "How's your car running?"

"I often wonder about that, Vern, because it's so old. But God keeps it running. He fills up the gas tank, too."

Vern smiles. "I thought I heard a squeaking sound when you drove up last night. Was that the windshield wipers again?"

"No. There are mice in my engine."

The Goldburgs laugh.

"It's not funny. They nest in there. They think it's warm, but it's only warm after it's been driven. They haven't figured that out yet. People don't think about mice that much, but they are destructive and ill-intentioned creatures."

"Vern and I will take a look at the car," Mr. G. volunteers. "Right, Vern?"

"Sure."

"You're a very nice man," Mom tells Mr. G. "You always have been. Miriam, do you know you're married to a nice man?"

"Yes, Eve."

"And handsome, too."

"Mom!" I glare at her.

"What is the matter with you, Sage? You keep saying 'Mom' but then there's nothing else. Teenage girls. They're always so embarrassed by their mothers, aren't they?"

Mrs. G. smiles. "Teenage boys, too. When they're young, they want all of your attention. Once they're past twelve, they want to hide you in the attic."

"I wouldn't hide you in the attic, Mom," Vern jokes. "It's too cold. Maybe in the den."

"Thank you, dear. That's comforting."

"Here is a joke," Sophie volunteers. "There's this guy and he's driving around a parking lot for an hour looking for a parking space. He's got an interview for an important job, and he's getting frustrated. So he makes a deal with God. He says, 'God, if you'll just find me a parking space, I'll never do anything bad again.' At that very moment, a parking space opens up right in front of him. 'Never mind, God,' the guy says. 'I just got a spot.'"

Mom clears her throat. "When you say 'God,' do you mean Jesus?"

"Uhm. No."

"Because God forsook his only son to die for our sins so that we would be saved for all eternity."

Sophie wrinkles up her face. "*My* God would never do that to his son. What kind of parent does that to their child?"

"And it was you Jews who killed him." Mom says it nonchalantly, like she expects everyone to nod and say, *Good point.*

"I don't see how you can say it was *us* Jews who killed Jesus." Mrs. G's voice is tense. "It's not like we were there. That's like saying, *You Germans exterminated us.* I mean, you have German blood, don't you, Eve? Wasn't your father German?"

"Yes, he was."

"I think it was the Romans who killed Jesus," Vern says. "If my history is correct."

"Besides," Sophie adds primly. "Jesus *was* Jewish."

Mom looks around the table. A hand goes up to her mouth, so that at least she has a clue she should keep it shut.

"Seconds, anyone?" Mr. G. says.

No one answers. I study the gold rim on my plate, and wonder if there will ever be a day in my life that I don't want something that someone else has: a normal mother, a job, a husband (Roger), children, my own house and dishes—they don't have to have gold on them, but maybe they could match.

All of a sudden, Mom stands up and rushes from the room like she's just remembered a vital appointment, then out the front door. We hear her footsteps on the walkway, then the car squealing out of the driveway.

There is a phrase in theater: a pregnant pause. It's a silence that says more than words.

"It's not the wipers that are squeaking." Vern finally breaks the silence. "I replaced those. And besides, it's not raining."

"The brakes, maybe," Mr. G. says.

Do not cry. Do not cry, I tell myself.

"I wonder where she went," Sophie says sadly.

"Maybe she had an errand she forgot," Mrs. G. says.

All of them are trying to make me feel better, which has the reverse effect. My papier-mâché face dissolves, and I start sobbing onto the beautiful tablecloth, the gold-rimmed china.

VERN

EVERYTHING IN THIS TOWN is being taken over by the chains. Jona's Great Java turned into a Dunkin' Donuts. Phil's Diner was knocked down to build a McDonald's. Book-it shut its doors after Borders came! The only holdover is Happy Diegos.

I took Sophie and Sage there last night, but neither was much company. Sophie wouldn't eat because it wasn't kosher. Sage is in her anorexia mode so all she had was a Diet Coke and a few chips. It may have been one chip that she broke into tiny pieces and nibbled.

Sage went on (and on) about Roger. She might as well have been throwing darts, with me as the dartboard. Clearly, he *is* trying to pick up on her.

Sophie talked about Yeshiva and the rabbi, who she seems to assume *is* God, rather than His humble and flawed servant.

What is it? The people I'm drawn to are all obsessives: Walter with architectural schemes, particle physics, and Kafka. Sophie and God. Sage and . . . her *life*!

It must be because I'm such a moderate. I'm wishy-washy. Yeah, I want to write, but I know I'll end up floating along the stream: law school, a good job, a family. I don't feel that strongly about anything. Just them: Mom and Dad, Sage, Sophie, Walter.

What we didn't talk about was Sage's mom, who seems to be after my dad in a big way. We stepped around the subject like dog poop on the sidewalk. I mean, *every* time he walks out the door, Eve appears and corners him. It's like she watches out the window. Once she gets him, she won't stop talking and flirting.

When we brought the Christmas tree over to them, Eve managed to hug my dad about twenty times, while ignoring me completely. The tree was my idea, after all.

Now both of my parents say they're selling the house as soon as I graduate. They've wanted to move for a long time—they can definitely afford better—but I've talked them out of it. Now they've had it; especially Mom. It's pretty tough watching someone trying to pick up your husband.

Sage also asked about Cassandra. God, I felt like such a joke riding around in that limo. The driver turned a blind eye when Cassie raided the minibar. By the time we got to the dance she was plastered, and all over me. And there I was, thinking about Sage the whole night, how much fun we would've had together.

Cassandra is not letting up. She's been hanging on

me at school like she's my girlfriend. It's weird; after years of being ignored by the chicks at school, I'm getting attention. And it's not just Cassandra. Mona Simms keeps talking to me in this shy way. All I did was congratulate her on the election and she gushed about what a good sport I was; like I really cared about the election. At least Mona's a nice girl. And smart.

After dinner (or *not* dinner for the girls), we walked to the end of the shopping center so I could get dessert, but the bakery was closed down and a dry cleaners is going in. Sage pressed her face against the window. I came up behind her and hugged her. Her hair smelled like leaves. Her skin is always warm, like she's been sitting by the fire.

"Maybe I can get a job there," she said.

When we got home, Sophie asked, "Do you want to marry Sage?"

I had to laugh. "Well, I wouldn't mind being her *boyfriend*."

"You're a boy and you're her friend."

"I mean, like, dating."

"I don't believe in dating," Sophie said. "Only marriage. I want an arranged marriage, so I don't have to worry about it."

"You'll let the rabbi choose?" I joked.

She frowned. "Maybe Mom and Dad, since they know me better."

My sister is from another century; that's for sure.

SAGE

CURRENT EVENTS. Ms. Carnal is reading newspaper clips aloud. She used to be a nun. Behind her back, the kids call her J. C. The J is for Jenna.

Ms. Carnal is drawn to the gruesome. The first clip was about people who steal jewelry from graves. The second was about a man who shot his baby with a stun gun when it cried. Now, for some reason, she's going on about George Foreman, the boxer. After he couldn't box, he became a Christian minister, then an entrepreneur selling grills. The weird part is that he named all five of his sons George. Talk about conceited.

Still, the name thing got me thinking. Your name does kind of mark you. Like Walter, being called Wal-Mart, to cheapen him.

In ancient times, a person's name actually was a secret. A name was like a voodoo doll in that way.

I need a new name, something that sounds thin and classy. Nothing lumbering or punk rock-y, like Pink Razor or Gutter Voice, names I might have taken with my old, goth image. Nora. Kind of like Mona. Nora Rockefeller. Katherine Vanderbilt.

After I graduate, I'll do it, change my name, find a way to go to college, buy nice clothes, and have a fridge full of food.

Speaking of Mona, she's in my new English class. Just seeing her makes me feel fat, clumsy, and stupid, despite my progress. Today she was wearing a full-length gray peacoat, a baby blue cashmere sweater, and an amazing scarf tied perfectly around her neck. I can never get scarves to look like that. They're always loose or there's an end dangling. God, her clothes make my mouth water.

I definitely have a clothes problem. If only someone would call me about a job. I've applied to, like, twenty places.

The bell rings for our new outdoor break. Principal Chard has decided that we need fresh air every day to wake up our slumbering minds. And light, so we don't get seasonal affective disorder (we actually had an assembly about this).

We're having a warm spell. It's about forty-five, which to a New Englander in winter feels like seventy. Good thing, too, since I'm wearing the pink dress yet again.

I do my Roger scan. Wherever he hangs out is a mystery to me. Maybe he sneaks off campus.

I look for someone to hang with. Being solo in high school is like having leprosy.

Fern and Reenie are smoking cigarettes behind the giant oak. "Hi, Sage," Reenie calls.

"I didn't know you smoked, Reenie."

"I just started. Weight control."

"Reenie was just telling me about her new car." Fern yawns.

"It's a RAV4," Reenie says.

"Christmas present?" I force a smile.

"Yeah." Reenie has *definitely* never been Sudan. "My dad took me to Bob Floyd Toyota to pick it out. I expected Bob Floyd would help me personally, like on the commercial. Instead, I got this old lady who stutters! I hate people who stutter. You can't understand what they're saying. Don't you hate that?"

"You know what I hate?" Fern points to a freshman walking by. "Guys with ponytails. They're so full of themselves. I want to grab them by their ponytail and say, 'You look stupid.'"

"What do you hate, Sage?" Reenie asks me.

"Hate?" *That we had a pot of chili for Christmas dinner, although Mom managed an iPod for me from God knows where, that Mom spent the whole day talking about the crucifixion of Jesus, and the enemies she has.* "Hunters."

"Me too," Fern goes. "They kill a little rabbit and think that makes them manly. You know what I would do if I found a hunter in my yard? I would take his gun and aim at him. I would scare the crap out of him so he'd know what it feels like."

"Roger Willis hunts." Reenie looks at me. "I saw him with his dad once; they had a dead deer strapped to the back of their truck."

Does Reenie know about my crush? "Maybe his dad did the shooting," I say.

"If he was with his dad, he was hunting too."

"I don't think he hunts."

"How would you know?" Reenie sounds snide.

Fern looks at Reenie, then me. "At least a guy with a ponytail is probably not a hunter. Those two things don't go together at all."

"No, the ponytail guy is probably an actor," I joke.

The bell rings. "That was *so* not ten minutes." Fern stomps out her cigarette and heads off.

"Fern is such a skank," Reenie says. "Do you really think she's from California? I'll bet she's from somewhere lame in the Midwest, like Idaho. Oh, there's Caroline. I gotta tell her about my RAV4."

"Idaho is not in the Midwest," I call after her, but she doesn't hear.

"There you are," *the* voice says behind me. "The invisible girl."

I turn to Roger and try to think of something amusing to say. Nothing comes.

"Cat got your tongue?" he says.

"I have a cat." *Lame-o!*

"Do you?"

"A black cat."

"Cute."

"Yeah, he's cute. But he's ancient."

"Are you cold?"

"No."

"You have goose bumps on your legs."

"Oh." *I got chills . . .*

"Me and your mom are getting to be good friends."

"My mom?"

"Didn't she tell you I called?"

Oh-mi-God. Oh-mi-God. "No!"

"I even spelled my name for her. R-o-g-e-r."

"My mom's a little weird."

"Mine's kind of weird too. She still thinks I'm seven years old."

"The bell rang," I say, instead of *I would like to spend my life with you!* "I better get to class."

"Take my jacket. Then you'll be warm. You can give it back to me after school." Roger puts his letterman jacket on my shoulders and tugs it around me.

"Thanks."

I float to history where Mr. Jess has already started a lecture on the French Resistance.

I'm so in my own world that it takes me a while to notice the kids whispering and pointing at me, or I should say, the jacket.

X X X X

After school, I look for Roger, but the halls are empty and his truck is gone. I walk home in a dream. Mom's car is in the driveway, so I go through the kitchen and hide the jacket in the bench. It's the kind of thing that could set her off.

The dream continues. The kitchen is clean. The house is warm. I go into the living room and see Mrs. G. stirring a fire with a poker. "Mrs. G.?"

It's only when she turns around and I see the tense smile and darting eyes, that I realize my mistake. "Mom?"

"You're late."

My mom has had her hair dyed red and either curled or permed. She's in new clothes, black slacks and a gray turtleneck. "What did you *do* to yourself?"

"You're not the only one who can get a makeover."

"With what money?"

"I went to the welfare office." She picks up an envelope. "We now have food stamps."

"So with money from the state, you got a makeover?"

"The social worker was a very nice lady. I think she was black or Mexican. Anyway, she had dark skin. She's going to visit us. She wants to meet you. They gave us medical, too. You can go to the doctor."

"Why would I go to the doctor?"

"At your age! For things like checkups and birth control."

"Birth control? Yeah, right."

"We don't need another mouth to feed. That's for sure."

"What are you *talking* about?"

"I'm talking about the boy you're sneaking out with."

"Vern?"

"Don't act innocent with me."

"You mean the boy who's been calling here that you never bothered to tell me about!" I'm yelling.

"You chased my boyfriend away, and besides, you are too young to talk to boys on the phone."

"I'm seventeen! I'll be eighteen in a couple of months!"

Mom steps back like I hit her. She looks me up and down, as if realizing only now that I'm not six. "Eighteen?"

"I have a right to my phone calls! There's nothing *else* going on in my life."

"Eighteen?"

"I guess you didn't notice that. You don't notice me at all. If you had, maybe you'd pick me up from school when it snows, instead of yelling at me because I'm late!" *Not that I really want her to, but it is ammunition.*

"I'm just telling you . . ." She gets quiet. "I have experience. I could tell by his voice; he's not very nice."

I hear a car pull into the Goldburg's driveway.

"I'm going outside to garden a bit," Mom says.

"In the snow?"

Mom grabs some gardening gloves and hedge clippers and rushes out the door. "Peter! Yoo-hoo . . ."

It all pulls together then: the hairdo, the clothes, the clean kitchen. She's even moving like her.

My mom wants to be Miriam Goldburg. She wants to be her so much.

More importantly, she wants her husband.

WAL-MART

True or false:

1. People who are popular in high school go on to have happy marriages, 2.5 children, and expensive cars. They do not become drug addicts, Internet abusers, sexual predators, or severe alcoholics (they become functional alcoholics). They do not have unwanted pregnancies, sexually transmitted diseases, or abortions, although they may stand in front of abortion clinics with graphic signs. They do not suffer from insomnia or lapses in judgment. They do not become psychotic; they become robotic.

2. Consuming a diet of Pop-Tarts, Twizzlers, and Necco Wafers can alter your sexual orientation and give you bad dreams.

3. Everyone is a celebrity.

SAGE

THAT DAY, when I got the jacket, I couldn't concentrate, because I knew that at some point Roger would want it back and I'd see him. At lunch, I looked for him, but he's wasn't in the cafeteria. Probably, he and his friends ate out. Or ditched. A lot of seniors do that.

When I got to the table, Vern's mouth dropped open. "So, have we committed a theft or just raided the Lost and Found?"

"It's Roger's," I gloated.

"I know." His voice was so soft I could barely hear it.

"He gave it to me to wear until, you know, after school."

"Have my lunch. I'm not hungry."

"That's okay. I'm not hungry either."

"What an odd coincidence."

✗ ✗ ✗ ✗

But I didn't see him. It's as if Roger is a magician who appears and disappears. I have to admit that there's part of me that wants to keep it, a consolation prize, something to sleep with at night, like when I was a kid and pretended my pillow was Bruce Springsteen.

I've dreamed my way through class every day, imagining the moment he takes it off my shoulders; how I'll lean in close, maybe even kind of hug him.

Today I'm determined to find him. As soon as classes let out, I hit the parking lot to see if he's still here. In Roger's space is Mona's Infiniti. Did he give her his spot? He must have.

The jacket meant nothing!

My heart is beating in a totally wild way. I can't believe how obsessed I feel.

I go back into the building. The halls are empty. I can't hear any action from the locker rooms. I feel like a lame-o standing around, so I go into the auditorium and find Madame T. She's sitting on the edge of the stage, probably thinking about how many Academy Awards she should've won in her lifetime.

"Hi, Madame T."

"In the 1970s, I was your age. I made my debut in *South Pacific* at the Loren Harding Theater in Newark, New Jersey. That was before Newark was such a craphole."

"I just wanted to pick up the script for *Grease*."

"The newspapers called me the most promising young actress to hit the stage since Debbie Reynolds. After that, I played Blanche in *Streetcar*."

"Uh, so where are the scripts?"

"On the desk. Black out all of the stage directions and highlight the parts in different colors on my copy by tomorrow."

A thank-you from her would be nice. "Okay." I sift through the pile of junk on her desk.

Reenie wanders in. "Hi, Madame T. I was just looking for the cast list."

"I took it down to make a couple of changes."

"Did I get a part?" Her voice is so shaky, I feel embarrassed for her.

"Not this time, Reenie. Sorry."

"But I'm a senior. I've been in the Thespians for four years, and you've never cast me in anything."

"That's because your voice is like mashed potatoes."

"What?"

"You don't enunciate."

Reenie starts to cry.

Madame T. looks up like she's finally noticed there are other human beings on the planet. "What's with you, Reenie?"

"How am I ever going to learn anything if you don't cast me?"

"Fine. Be in the chorus. You'll look all right in bobby socks."

"Thank you, Madame T."

"Sage," she orders. "A script for Reenie."

I grab a script and bring it over.

"I didn't see you." Reenie's face goes red.

"That's because stage managers are supposed to be invisible. Congrats."

"Yeah. Right."

✗ ✗ ✗ ✗

Back outside, it's gray and freezing. If I'd left after school, I could've hitched a ride with Vern. I have to stop being so stupid! A watched pot never boils. A desperate girl never gets the guy. That's the thing about Mona. She seems like she doesn't care.

But then, like magic, he appears. "Hey, I've been looking for you. You've still got my jacket, I see." Roger's hair is wet and kind of frozen to his head.

"Sorry. I couldn't find you to give it back."

"Need a ride?"

"Sure."

"I was late this morning and some idiot was parked in my space, so I had to park on the street."

That idiot was Mona, I want to tell him. She drives a brand-new silver Infiniti. I'm surprised he doesn't know that. "Your hair has turned to ice."

"Yeah." He grins. "I should dry it before I go outside."

We walk through the parking lot to the street, where

his truck is parked. He opens the door for me, or sort of for both of us, because the driver's side is wired shut and he has to get in on the passenger side.

As he starts the car, my eyes go right to the dash. Mona is gone. The tape is still there, but no picture, like a clear frame around nothing. I feel a grin spread on my face.

"You live on Southwest. Right?"

"How'd you know?"

"It wasn't easy. You're not listed in the phone book."

"I know." *Mom's paranoia.*

"So I went into the coach's computer and got your school record."

"Oh." *I hope he didn't look at my grades.*

"What a cool name. Sage Priestly. You half expect your dad to be the Pope." He is so funny and cute and popular! "But your mom . . . Already she doesn't like me."

"She's just . . ."

"Strict?"

"Yeah." *Well, actually, crazy.*

"I got that impression. Like no-guy-is-good-enough-for-my-daughter kind of thing."

"Yeah." *Find something else to say!*

"How about your dad?"

"Well, he's not the Pope." I giggle. "He lives some-where else, another state. I don't know where."

"So your mom's a single mom? That's why she's strict. Single parents always feel like they have to compensate."

"Are your parents together?"

"Oh, yeah. They're that type. Apple pie. Bowling league. Church. The whole American dream."

"Great!"

"That's how it should be." He lays his hand over mine. I melt like a puddle of butter on a pancake. "Did you know that wearing a guy's jacket means you're going out with him?"

"Uh . . ."

"That's what it means. If it's okay with you."

"It's okay." My voice comes out squeaky.

"We could pick up some burgers Saturday and then go to the park. That be okay?"

It's nice the way he asks, so respectful. "Yeah." *A whole vocabulary of one word.*

"You're so pretty."

Oh-mi-God! It's like life giving me crepes instead of scrambled eggs. For once.

He pulls up in front of my house.

"Thanks for the ride."

"No problem. Do you mind if I take my jacket back? I've got to run errands and the heat doesn't work in my truck."

Actually, I do. "No. Sure. Here."

He tugs the jacket off my shoulders. I try to think of something to say to make the whole thing last longer, to make sure it's not a dream. But he's looking past me. "Your house is on fire!"

"Huh?" I jerk my head around; orange flames are shooting up around the kitchen window. Roger tries to open his door, but since it's wired shut, he can't get out.

"Wait here!" I shout, and rush in the kitchen door. Mom is standing with a cigarette in her hand, watching the flames crawl up the curtains. I turn on the sink and aim the sprayer at the fire. It takes about thirty seconds to extinguish it.

"I don't know what happened," Mom says. "I was just lighting my cigarette."

"Were you going to stand here and watch the house burn down?" I yell, but then I remember Roger. He's almost to the steps when I reach him. "It's okay!" I tug him toward his truck. "No big deal. Just a frying-pan fire."

"Are you sure it's out?"

Kelly Easton

"Yeah. I'm sure. No problem."

"We should call the fire department. Sometimes fires reignite."

"It's totally out. My mom and her friend were just frying something," I lie, "and water got in with the oil. Then they moved the pan to the sink and it caught the curtains."

"I volunteer with the fire department in the summer. Why don't I go check it out?"

"No!" I grab his arm. "Her boyfriend's there. He's taking care of it."

He pulls me in close. "Do me a favor."

"What?"

"Check the batteries on your smoke detectors. I didn't hear anything going off."

"Okay."

Vern comes out then and walks to their mailbox. I can tell he's watching us. I also know that Sophie always brings the mail in right after school.

"What's *he* doing there?" Roger glares at him.

"Vern lives there."

"Next door to you?"

"Always has."

"Steer clear of him," he says. "I've never liked that creep."

VERN

TONIGHT, Walter and I took the train into Boston, to an art house that was playing *Pulp Fiction.*

The John Travolta character's guts were scattered in one scene. In the next, he's back, grinning like a moron. Time and space were fractured in the film; that was the gimmick.

Everybody said this film was so cool, but I could hardly stomach it. Everything teenagers think is cool, sucks: violent movies, reality TV, YouTube, skinny girls, designer clothes, bottled water, iPods, TiVo, Wii, texting. Facebook sucks. Loud, drunken parties suck. Football sucks. All team sports. Dates suck, especially with someone who annoys you. Roger Willis sucks. Big time.

Sage is going out with that moron.

If I hadn't taken Cassandra to the dance, then Sage would never have gone over to him in the first place.

Time and space. Blood and guts. One false move. That's what they say in movies. You make one false move . . . and it's over.

SAGE

TALK ABOUT A DIET TOOL. I've barely eaten since Roger asked me out. "You can't live on love," Mr. G. tells Sophie when she's picky about eating. But maybe you can.

Selfish and I are reading *Slaughterhouse-Five*, which I'm supposed to finish by Monday. I'm trying not to watch the clock; Roger was supposed to be here fifteen minutes ago.

Vonnegut's an amazing writer, but I can't concentrate. I've read the same sentence five times: "They studied the infinitesimal effects of spit on snow and history." If Vern could come up with a line like that, he'd die happy.

My plan is to run out the door as soon as he drives up, before Mom has a chance to notice. I'm almost eighteen. As far as I'm concerned, I can do what I want.

"Sage!" she calls. "There's nothing in the fridge. Did you spend all the food stamps?"

"Eat the curtains. They've been fried." I still haven't had the nerve to use the food stamps. The idea of being seen is too depressing.

Mom appears in the doorway. She's looking less like Mrs. Goldburg. Her hair is a mess and she's back to the 1950s clothes. "What are you reading?"

"Something for school." I'm starting to worry that he's not showing up.

"When you were little I used to read to you. Do you remember? You liked *The Teddy Bears' Picnic*, Dr. Seuss, and books about trains. Sometimes, I read you poems I'd written. Most were about the sky. One was about the way constellation rhymes with consolation. I thought that was a good connection to make. I had such energy then. I felt like electricity was in my blood, like someone had plugged me into the wall. Sometimes I couldn't sleep, I had such amazing thoughts. Robert snored when he slept. He didn't have amazing thoughts. He just wanted to find a way to use the barbecue in the winter. He wanted to score good seats for the Red Sox game, and have a job that paid well and didn't have overtime."

"The good old days," I say nervously, standing up to block her view of the window. "The food stamps are in the kitchen drawer. We need coffee and cheddar and the creamer you like."

"Why didn't you say so?" She goes into the kitchen. "Which drawer?"

"By the fridge." I hear Roger's truck. Excitement rushes through me like a drug.

"I'll go see if the newspaper came," I call, my heart pounding.

"We don't get the newspaper."

"Maybe they started delivering it." I dart out the door and jump into his truck. "Drive," I say. "Before my mom changes her mind about me going."

He pulls away from the curb. "Boy, she is strict. Sorry I kept you waiting. We had a recruiting meeting. I was helping the coach pick the freshman team. It's pretty sad to be doing that after all these years, hiring your own replacements. Man, if I could stay in high school forever, I would do it."

Stay in high school forever? Sounds like purgatory, maybe even hell. "Me too," I say.

"I'm starving. Burger King or Wendy's? First date. You pick."

I've never been in either. "Burger King."

"Okay, but I like Wendy's better."

"Go there, then. It doesn't matter to me."

"God, you wouldn't believe the pathetic recruits. Coach Walker was so depressed. They were total wimps. I'm like, 'Where's the beef?' You could snap their necks just by tackling 'em. What an embarrassment that's going to be."

Roger is beefy. Muscles are practically bulging out of his shirt. I still can't believe I'm with him.

x x x x

As we step into the restaurant, the smell of burgers, fries, and cleaning fluid makes me nauseous.

"What do you want?" he asks.

"I'll just have a Diet Coke."

"You girls are always dieting."

"I ate a big lunch," I lie.

The girl at the counter leans toward him. "Hi, Rog. Let me guess. Large fries. Big Classic Triple with extra ketchup. Chili. Baked potato. Large chocolate shake."

Has her picture ever been taped up on the dash?

"You got it." He grins. "Uh, what did you say you wanted, Sage?"

"Diet Coke."

"What size?" the girl asks.

"Medium." She shoves an empty cup at me.

"Six eighty." She winks at Roger. "I'll bring it to you when it's ready."

"Yours is a dollar forty-nine." Roger puts out his hand.

"Huh?"

"The Diet Coke."

I really could throw up; I feel so stupid. I assumed

that he would buy it for me, which is so lame. It's probably because Vern always pays when we go out. But Vern knows I don't have money and Roger doesn't. I mean, this is, like, the twenty-first century. Boys and girls both pay. "Oh, sorry. I'm really sorry, but I forgot my wallet. I was kind of rushing to get out of the house."

"So, take off the Diet Coke?" the girl says.

"No," Roger says. "It's cool."

Thank God. I would feel so stupid if I didn't have anything to eat or drink. "I'm just going to use the ladies' room."

"I'll get your drink." He takes the cup.

I go into the bathroom and lock myself in the stall. Maybe I should just stay here. Become a homeless person who lives in the Wendy's lavatory. It makes me understand my mom a bit, the way she avoids reality, avoids life. It's less anxiety-provoking.

I splash cold water on my face and brush my hair, trying to fluff it up so the roots don't show. I practice my Mona smile and launch myself back into the real world.

When I get to the table, he's already eaten half the burger and is starting on the chili. He's also on his cell phone. "Dude, I'll be there, like . . ." He looks at his watch. "Ten. Forget it. Yeah. It's cool. Gotta eat. Gotta go."

I feel a little insulted he didn't say, *Gotta go, my girlfriend is here.*

"Remember when this chick found a finger in her chili, then tried to sue Wendy's?" he says. "They did scientific tests on the finger and found out it was not in the chili for any length of time. It was her friend's finger, as it turns out. I hope she's in jail a long time."

"Yeah. Really." I pray for words with more than one syllable to enter my brain.

"I love to see people get their just desserts. Don't you?"

"Most of the time, it seems the opposite. Bad things happen to people who don't deserve it." I take a sip.

"I got you regular," Roger says. "Diet tastes like crap."

"Oh."

"Want a bite?" He lifts the burger to me. The meat resembles a decaying sponge. Ketchup squeezes out like blood.

"That's okay."

"I know. Dieting."

"Not really."

"You don't need to diet. You look good a little chubby. It makes your cheeks round."

I am never eating anything again as long as I live. "Thanks," I mutter.

"First time I saw you in the cafeteria, that was my second thought: cute cheeks. Know what my first was?"

"Clumsy hands?"

"Ha. Very funny. Great legs."

I smile and wish I'd worn a skirt.

His phone rings; the national anthem. "Yo!" I can tell it's one of his football buddies, because he talks in a male code, one syllable words, numbers that must be scores. I see other people walking back to the fountain with their empty cups, so I guess you're allowed to refill. I go over, discreetly empty my cup, and fill it with Diet Coke. When I come back, he's off the phone and back at his burger. "You know the secret of playing football? Of having the strength to power through a game?"

"No."

"Meat. Any kind. But I especially love venison. Some day, people will get Bambi out of their brains and places like this will serve it."

"So, you hunt?"

"Sure. Come on. Have a bite. You can never have too much ketchup."

Ketchup is to cuisine what the romance novel is to literature, but I don't want to insult him. "Okay." I bite. It's about as disgusting as I imagined. "So," I ask, "who's that girl at the counter? She looked familiar."

"Lori Rivera. She graduated last year. One of the few who didn't go to college."

Did you go out with her? "Was she a cheerleader?"

"Nah, she hung with a rougher crowd. She asked me out, but my crowd didn't hang with her crowd so it wouldn't be cool."

I wonder what crowd he thinks I hang with. "I kind of hang out with the theater kids," I admit.

"Yeah, Al told me. I usually wouldn't want to be seen with one of those Thespian dorks, but you're different. You're not all playing-at-eccentricity or showing off. Besides, you hang with Fern and Reenie and they're pretty cool. They belong to, like, every group."

"Vern's like that." It slips out before I remember he doesn't like him. "He hangs with everyone."

"Did you go out with him or something?"

"No."

"That's good, because it would look pretty bad for me to go out with someone who dated that loser."

I'm beginning to think of this as the evening of the upset stomach. "Why don't you like him?"

"He's friends with that faggot Wal-Mart, for one thing. That makes him totally suspect in my book."

"Oh."

His phone rings again. This time, I'm glad, because the Wal-Mart comment has made me speechless.

To whoever it is, he says, "Henry Ford didn't go to college. Edison didn't go to college. Neither did Sam Walton or Bill Gates. It's just marketing, convincing kids that their lives will be a failure if they don't sit in a bunch of lectures for hours to give nerds a paycheck. Twelve years is enough. Just stand your ground. Your dad'll cave. Hey, I gotta go." He hangs up. "Sorry. Some people can't think for themselves, you know."

"So, you're not going to college."

"I'm going to Police Academy, to be a cop. I actually saw a bank being robbed once."

"You're kidding."

"My dad and me were in Boston, going to a hockey game. We went into the bank to get some cash. No big deal. Then there's, like, a gun pointed at us and we're told to get on the floor facedown."

"Weren't you scared?"

"I should've been. But I was fascinated. And I was

pissed, too, because no one makes my dad lay on the ground. But my dad did and he pulled me down with him. There were two of them and while one pointed guns at us, the other took money from the teller. Then they were gone. When my dad got up, he was so pissed. He smacked me."

"Why?"

"Because I kept looking up. I was so curious. He said I could've gotten us killed." Roger shrugs. "There's two kinds of people. You can already see that in high school. Good and bad. I'm gonna be a cop and cleanse out the bad guys. Old-fashioned?"

"No," I say, but the word "cleanse" is kind of freaky. It sounds so . . . Aryan.

"A lot of girls don't want to marry a cop, because they figure cops have a higher chance of getting killed, but it's not that bad. Not in this state, anyway. But you'd marry a cop, wouldn't you?" He leans forward and kisses me, his arms wrapping around me. He's so warm and big, like a bear. I can't believe he's talking about marriage on the first date.

"Yes," I whisper.

He kisses me again, his mouth tasting like ketchup.

I wonder what he sees in me.

VERN

FIVE IN THE MORNING. Don't know how long I've been awake. I was having a dream—no, a nightmare—about Cassie, that she was on a TV show. The set was a bedroom with hokey furniture, like out of a sitcom. I was watching, but then she noticed me, and dragged me onto the set. The lights were blinding. "Come on, Vernie," she urged. "Get into the bed."

The director started yelling at me to hurry and take off my clothes so they could shoot the scene. When I explained to him that I wasn't the actor, but the writer of the show, he started laughing. Then they all laughed. "You?" they said. "The writer?"

I woke up to this scratching sound. At first, I thought maybe a mouse was trapped inside the walls. But then I realized it's outside. I've lain here for ten minutes, listening. This house is so badly insulated.

Finally, I get up and go to the window. In the moonlight, I can see Sage's mom outside in her nightgown and slippers. She's dragging a bucket on the sidewalk. I think it's a bucket of chalk. And she's writing something.

When she finally goes inside, I go out to have a look. In purple, pink, and yellow chalk, Eve has written over and over on the sidewalk: JESUS SAVES.

I know Sage will be nuts when she sees it, so I go inside and fill a pail with water.

Mom's already to the coffeemaker before she notices me. "Vern, what are you doing up?"

I tell her about the writings. She grabs a couple of sponges, puts on her coat, and follows me out. It takes only a few minutes to wash the chalk off. We're almost done when Eve appears, her hair all crazy, her nightgown on backward. No robe or coat.

"Filthy pigs!" she yells.

"Go back to bed," Mom orders. "I'll bring you some breakfast later."

"Okay, Miriam." She goes back inside.

"Did you see those curtains in the trash can?" Mom says.

"Uh, yeah."

"They're all burned up."

"I think there was . . . a small fire there."

Mom gets her lawyer look. "When was that?"

"A couple of weeks ago."

"Odd that you didn't mention it."

"Sage put it out. It's okay."

"That's it!"

"What?"

"All these years I've wanted to get her some help, to make her see a psychiatrist, and to protect that poor girl."

"We've been here. We've protected Sage."

"The house could've burned down. And what about Eve? What kind of life is she living? She needs help."

"You're just mad 'cause she's after Dad," I joke, but the look she gives me lets me know it's not funny.

"I wish Robert hadn't left."

"Why did he?"

"This." She motions to the sidewalk. "This is why he left. He was the target of her craziness. One time, he bought a new car. Since it was blue, Eve raged and screamed at him that she'd wanted a green car and he should've known it. The poor guy. You should've seen the way his face fell. Then Eve drove off in it."

"And?"

"When she got back, the car was a mess. It looked like she'd driven it through a muddy swamp. The fender was smashed. One of the doors was dented."

"Oh, it's *that* car."

"Yes, the same car they have now. Three weeks later, he left. He came over and told us he had a job offer in Oklahoma and he was taking it. 'What's going to happen to Sage?' I asked him. Robert said, 'Eve never goes after Sage. She adores her. I'm the one who gets her mad. I can't do anything right.'"

"Was it true?"

"She screamed and threw things at Robert, but Sage was the apple of her eye. She wasn't abusive to Sage."

"So he just walked out? What a coward."

"That's how I saw it."

"Did you ever hear from him again?"

"For a few years, he wrote. Work was going well. He met someone. He remarried, moved to Texas, had a baby. But the letters became less frequent, then finally stopped."

"You never told me this stuff before."

"Who needs to think about it?" She covers her face with her hands. "I'm going to get Eve seen somewhere. She told Dad she has a social worker. She may need to be hospitalized. Sage can stay with us."

"Sage barely talks to me anymore."

"Why not?"

I shrug. I'm past the age where I want to spill my guts to Mommy, although it's tempting. "She's *busy*."

SAGE

YESTERDAY WAS OUR first rehearsal of *Grease*. It went smoothly because the music teacher is working with the cast right now, and not Madame T. (who really takes the *fun* out of dys*fun*ctional).

Since I've been going out with Roger, I'm getting all of this attention. It's like, for the first time in my life, I'm part of things, rather than this poor kid with her face pressed to the window, watching. Like at lunch, Audrey Stewart and Jenna Li (head cheerleader!) invited me to sit with them. I was two seats away from Mona.

I felt mean not sitting with Vern, but Roger hates it when I'm with Vern. He says it looks like I'm cheating on him.

Anyway, tonight is my fifth date with Roger! I have a boyfriend! I'm practically dancing home. I walk in my front door and the house is warm once again. There's the smell of food cooking.

Selfish is asleep in the kitchen sink. I pick him up, then lift the lid off the pot on the stove. There's brisket, potatoes, and gravy. Now she's even imitating Mrs. G.'s cooking.

"Hello, dear." A sneeze.

"Oh, Mrs. G.! It really *is* you."

"Hmm?"

"I thought you were Mom. Where is she?"

"She's . . . uh, out. That is, I took her to the doctor this afternoon and they decided to keep her."

"Keep her?"

"In the hospital."

"Is she sick?"

"No, don't worry. It's a mental hospital."

"A mental hospital? What did she do now?"

"Nothing. I just talked to her and we decided to go to the doctor. Peter went too. That was the only way she'd go, if *he* went. We both took off work. . . ."

"Oh." As much as I love Mrs. G., it feels intrusive that she's done this without talking to me.

"I—we—just decided to check in with her today and she, well, she wasn't doing very well."

"But she's never doing well. There's nothing unusual about that."

"She gave me permission to call her social worker— nice lady—who hooked us up with a doctor."

"What hospital is she in?"

"It's the state hospital, Sage. In Providence."

"What's it like? People strapped to their beds, ranting and raving?"

"It's not like that. We were there for almost three hours . . . going over everything with the doctor: her behaviors, the way she feels. Your mom was very cooperative, and relieved. We have a diagnosis, Sage." She says it like she's giving me a gift.

"A diagnosis?"

"The doctor was absolutely certain, given her history. And with a diagnosis, there's treatment."

"What is the diagnosis?"

"Bipolar disorder. Sometimes it's called manic depression."

Hearing those words, something clicks in my brain, like a puzzle piece snapping into place. Manic depression. The extreme swings in her mood from crazed excitement to flattened misery.

"It's all in the brain chemistry. It's not her fault any more than if she had asthma or diabetes or allergies." She sneezes. "The cat . . . speaking of allergies."

"How do people get this?"

"It's just there, you know. In the brain . . . sort of waiting to come forth at some age and time. There is . . . a hereditary element."

"Great."

"That doesn't mean you'll have it. You might just want to be aware, that's all, when you get older. And it's completely treatable with medication. She'll be able to live normally."

"Normally?" That doesn't seem possible. Mrs. G. sneezes again. I pick up Selfish.

"It's covered by Medicaid. Everything. Thank God she'd gone to Social Services."

"How long will she be there?"

"Just until the medications are balanced and her mood stabilized."

"Can she get out? I mean, if she wants to."

"She committed herself. No one forced her."

"But she can't get out until the doctor lets her."

"That's right."

"I don't think she should be locked up." My voice comes out angry.

"Don't shoot the messenger."

"Can I go see her?"

"There are visiting hours, but the doctor says it's best to let patients adjust to being there before you visit. It can be upsetting and make them want to leave. You can call her any time. And the social worker. Her name is Mrs. Grove. She's going to come and see you. She wanted you to be placed in foster care. . . ."

"What?" I freak out. "I'm going to be eighteen next month!"

She waves me off. "I told her you could stay with us."

I look at the clock. Roger will be here in an hour. My whole life, I've wanted nothing more than to live with the Goldburgs. But if I was staying there, Roger would go nuts. He'd think I was with Vernon, for real.

"Thanks, Mrs. G., but I'd better stay here so I can take care of Selfish. You're allergic to him."

"You can just come over and take care of him."

"I mean, he sleeps in my bed and everything."

"I'd feel better if you stayed with us."

"I'll be fine. You're right there if I need you."

"True." Mrs. G. looks at her watch. She has a *life*, places to be. Will Mom now be able to have a life? "I have a meeting. I'm sorry."

"It's okay."

"Sage."

"Yeah?"

"Is everything okay between you and Vern?"

"Sure. Vern's my best friend. I'm just in rehearsals and stuff. Really busy."

"Dinner's there, if you're hungry."

"Thanks, Mrs. G. You're the best."

"I'm glad you still think so." She's out the door like I've insulted her.

✗ ✗ ✗ ✗

I don't tell Roger about Mom being "away." When he talks about his family, they sound so normal. His mom does needlework. His dad is a colonel in the navy. They're Republicans, which is creepy, but I can deal with that. I mean, Mom hasn't voted in years, so who's to talk.

Besides, he might want to come in. The house is so embarrassing: the couch with the spring sticking out, the filthy carpet, Mom's piles of junk. Also, he wants to *do more* than just kiss. It's becoming a major pressure.

Just when he pulls up, the phone rings. I almost don't answer it, but what if it's Mom or the social worker?

"Sage Priestly?" Like I'm either in trouble or have won a prize.

"Yes?"

It's the drugstore inviting me for a job interview on Saturday. Roger's honking the horn; it sounds like he's right in my living room. I wave at him that I'll be right there, but he keeps honking. I tell the woman I'll be there and hang up.

I run out and climb in. "Sorry."

"I almost drove off."

"Didn't you see me wave? I got a call for a job interview at CVS. The lady said, 'Oh, Miss Priestly, I knew your mom back in high school when we were just girls. She was so popular and vivacious.' Isn't that funny? I never think about my mom as being the popular type."

"No, *you* wouldn't."

"What do you mean?" My voice comes out scared.

He pats my leg. "I didn't know your mom grew up here."

"Yeah. Her whole life."

"So when's this job interview?"

"Saturday, at two."

"But we're going to the baseball game Saturday. It's the first day of the season."

"We are?"

"I told you last night on the phone. The game starts at one-thirty."

"I don't remember you asking me to a baseball game." I would definitely remember that.

"It's Al's league."

"Why don't I meet you after? I've applied to a million places and this is the first interview I've gotten."

"Why would you want to work at CVS? Andrew Weller and Carl Crowl work there. All the dweebs. You know they'll try to pick up on you."

I'm about to correct him. Like, I'm not the type who gets picked up on. But then I realize that it's kind of flattering that he worries about it. "It'll be okay."

"Don't come if you're going to miss the beginning of the game. You know how baseball is. If you miss part of the first inning, you're lost."

"Really?"

"Yeah. Plus, I already told my buddies you were coming, so I'm going to look like a moron."

He has never brought me anywhere with his buddies. Even at lunch, he sits with the guys and I sit with the girls. "I'll try to reschedule the interview. It just doesn't seem like a great way to impress a future employer."

"That's my girl." *My girl.* I feel like pinching myself, that the best-looking and most popular boy in school likes me.

"I can't wait to kiss you." He pulls into the park and shuts off the engine. Immediately, he's all over me, an octopus on caffeine.

I should be enjoying myself, but I'm not. I'm thinking about Mom and wondering if she's scared, and I'm realizing I didn't talk to Roger yesterday. I didn't see him at school and he didn't call. So when did he invite me to the game?

WAL-MART

THE OPENING LINE OF *THE METAMORPHOSIS*: "When Gregor Samsa woke up one morning from unsettling dreams, he found himself transformed into a monstrous vermin." The vermin is, by all accounts, a cockroach.

The irony in Kafka's story is that Gregor Samsa has been living his life like a cockroach all along, an automaton, a cog in the wheel, without contemplation or expression, without *being*.

Timeless story. Only now it's computers and TV and "fitting in." The world overrun by cockroaches.

✗ ✗ ✗ ✗

Today's shrink wears a red shirt and looks like a punk rocker. His name is Andy. Just Andy. He doesn't call himself Dr. this or that.

Bernstein recommended him when I had a meltdown in his office about the hypothetical questions. Bernstein is gay, I'm guessing. One gay recognizes another. But I wouldn't mention it to anyone; not even Vern. It's Bernstein's business. "It's been hilarious to watch everyone go nuts over these questions," Bernstein said. "I couldn't have thought them up myself. But it's cool. You doing okay?"

"Never," I said.

"I know someone you could see, if you want."

"That's okay."

"Getting a good therapist is like finding a needle in a haystack, I know. But he's really good."

"Maybe." It's the first time I *asked* my mom to take me to a shrink.

x x x x

Andy grabs Mom's hand and shakes it. "Hello, Mrs. Martin."

I can see her flinching at his appearance, his spiky hair and red shirt. If she could, she would drag me home. "I think I'll just sit in a little on this session," she says.

"The first session, I just talk to the teens by themselves, if that's okay with you. Then, later, when they feel comfortable, they invite you in to, you know, hear their thoughts. It just lets them . . . be in control of the process."

"Well . . ." Mom has this massive purse. It's like a giant mouth. She keeps, among other things, my dad's ashes in there.

She opens and closes the purse, like there's an excuse in there that she can pull out. She's from Ohio. Maybe that's her problem. She thinks that to be American is to be white, straight, and slightly overweight, to watch

America's Funniest Home Videos, to listen to *Prairie Home Companion*, and to vacation at Disney World. "Do you want me to come in, Walter?" She finally pulls out a tissue.

"Nah," I say.

Andy and I go into his office. It's weird, but immediately, I trust the guy. It's like the way I felt when I saw Vern in PE that first day of middle school.

"Start with what seems most important to you," he says.

Immediately, images come to me of certain episodes. I've never thought of them as the root of my depression or anything: my dad's death when I was ten; having my artwork defaced at school, the word FAG in black paint scrawled across all six of my paintings; the numerous times I was ambushed in the locker room, including the worst time when Roger Willis, Al Smith, and Dave Charney shoved the underpants in my mouth and tried to stick me into a locker. Vern made the lights go out in the whole school so I could escape.

If it weren't for Vern's friendship, I would've killed myself for sure.

I tell him how I've tried to come out to Mom and what a fiasco it's been each time.

Andy doesn't talk much. He doesn't *try*.

He just nods his head and goes, "Been there."

"You have?"

"Been there. Yeah. I have." And I feel less like a cockroach. Because he's sitting there in his amazing art deco office, looking totally comfortable with himself. "It gets better. Swear to God, it does. Once you get the hell out of high school."

SAGE

LAST WEEK'S FLUFFY snow has turned to glass. Running, I slipped several times. Thank God there was no one around to see me looking like all three of the Stooges.

The loop around the park is four miles. When we were little, Vern and I used to sled on the hill by the playground. I rode on the back. "You on?" he'd ask every time.

I'd squeeze him tight.

I remember one winter, Mom took us ice skating. I was surprised she had her own skates. Then, while Vern and I stumbled and clutched each other, Mom took off across the ice: gliding, spinning, and jumping. She was so amazing. "Wow, I didn't think I could still do that," she said. But I felt angry, because there was something I didn't know, a life she'd lived before. That was when we were still close.

"You're fantastic," Vern complimented her.

"Thank you." Mom smiled.

I looked away. I didn't say anything.

I've often wondered if it was me that made her crazy. My being difficult or . . . something. But no, it's "brain chemistry." And a pill will make her normal again?

I haven't gotten to visit her yet. On the phone, she sounded flat and tired. She kept repeating over and over, "I'm okay," like she was trying to convince me, or maybe herself.

I've got to stop obsessing. Just step into the shower and wash it all away. Focus on the positive. The present. Seven forty-five and I've jogged and finished my paper on *Slaughterhouse-Five*.

Great book. The main character, Billy Pilgrim, travels to another planet. Aliens capture him and keep him in a zoo. Vonnegut's aliens are called Tralfamadorians. Instead of the usual literary analysis, I created my own aliens. They have eyes in their chests, and mouths on their butts. Their many hands come out of the tops of their heads, like Medusa's snakes.

When they comment on our planet, they giggle with sour mirth. *The Bush Presidency*, they might say. *Ha ha ha. Congressional integrity. Ha ha ha. Social justice. Ha* . . . laughing so hard that they finally have to sit down to cover their mouths. I hope Bernstein doesn't mind my weird approach. He told us to "be creative."

The house is freezing.

Focus on the positive. In fifteen minutes, my boy-friend (!) is taking me out for coffee, then to school.

So why don't I feel positive?

In English, Bernstein said that Americans operate on a "carrot on a stick" mentality, chasing one desire, then another. He was no longer talking about *Slaughterhouse-Five*, but the next book we have to read: *Siddhartha*, about the life of Buddha.

As for my own carrot, I still want Roger. It's just that there are days when the idea of going out with him makes me tired. He wants to drive around in his unheated truck, park, and *octopus* (my new verb). It takes a lot of effort to keep my clothes on. The only time I get a break is when his cell phone rings. And he always answers it!

Also, I feel unsettled when I'm with him, the way I do with Mom, when I'm not sure if she's going to sit down for dinner or knock all the dishes off the table.

He wants control over me. Is that love? Was my dad like that with my mom?

Maybe relationships are like going on a cruise: glamorous at first, but then a tad claustrophobic.

It was different with Vern. We went to restaurants, to movies and concerts, to the beach. We could talk nonstop or be quiet, and it would be *comfortable*.

But he wasn't my boyfriend. Maybe he and Cassie just make out too. Hard to imagine Vern not being bored by that.

Every time I see Vern, I feel guilty. Roger made such a big deal about my friendship with Vern that I've drifted away.

I throw on my jeans and the blue sweater I found at Salvation Army, then my best score, a pair of beat-up, used-to-be-beige Uggs. A size too big, but they're Uggs!

Deep breath. Check the mirror. My roots are majorly showing now. Dark circles under my eyes. Some cheekbone action. Jeans loose. But I don't *look* thin. With this round face, I never will.

I'd better see if he's here. Roger hates to wait.

In the kitchen, Selfish winds himself around my legs. He has a sixth sense for when I feel upset. "Hungry?"

He purrs. The house is so silent. I miss my mom. Who would have thought?

I give him an extra large scoop of cat food. "Sorry, I don't have the canned." They don't let you buy pet food with food stamps.

Selfish sniffs the dry food and walks away, his tail up, which is his way of telling me off.

Now it's eight o'clock. If Roger doesn't come soon, we'll have to skip Starbucks. I even scraped up change for a coffee. But I should always remember the "Roger Factor," meaning, he's *always* late.

I grab my backpack and the goodies I baked and head outside, as if that will make him come sooner.

He could use his cell phone to call; it rings enough when we're together. Wow, I'm madder than I thought.

February is the most depressing month. Winter feels like a terminal illness. The conversation in the halls is about colleges and more colleges. Bernstein says I'd better apply and should major in English. He might as well tell me to go to Tralfamadore.

Roger drives up and honks his horn, even though I'm standing right here. I can tell he's in a bad mood, because he doesn't look at me or say hi as I get into the car.

"I made you butterscotch melts." I set them on the seat between us. "I was so busy with my paper last night, I almost burned them, but I think they're okay."

He accelerates, staring at the road in front of him.

"I love working with butterscotch. It's like toffee, except you add lemon. You can't taste the lemon, but it's there. So many foods were invented during hard times. Like toffee was invented in England when molasses was cheap. Divinity fudge was invented during the war when sugar was scarce and corn syrup was substituted. It's kind of out of fashion now."

"And the point is?" His voice is hard.

"N-nothing. It's just . . . something to talk about."

"Why does food interest you so much, anyway? You never eat. Or are you one of those girls who eats when no one's looking, then throws up?"

"I eat," I say defensively, but right now I do feel like throwing up. "Are you mad at me or something?"

"No."

"I don't get why you're being so—"

"Can't you take a joke?"

Not when the joke is at my expense.

Roger takes a sharp left, away from the school.

"Where are you going?"

"Starbucks."

"But we're already late. I'm going to miss my math test."

"I'll go to drive through."

"We'll get detention."

"Coach Collins never makes me serve detention."

"I don't have Coach Collins."

"We're here, so we might as well order. Do you want anything?"

"Coffee. Black."

"One diet coffee, tall," he calls into the speaker, "and a mocha latte."

"A diet coffee?" The voice has an accent. "What is a diet coffee?"

"Black!" He pulls forward to the window. "These people should learn to speak English."

"Yours is a dollar sixty." He holds out his hand. "In my dad's day, coffee was ten cents and you got unlimited refills."

"Yeah, but it tasted like dishwater." I give him the money.

"Here. Careful, it's hot." He says it gently, like he likes me again. "So, where were you last night? I called and you didn't answer."

"I was home. When did you call?"

"A bunch of times, around seven or eight."

"No one called."

"It just rang and rang."

"I was right there, doing my homework."

"Maybe the phone was off the hook."

"The phone wasn't off the hook. I had other calls." *Fern wanting me to go take drugs somewhere, and my mom sounding drugged.*

"I don't need to be interrogated."

"I'm not interrogating. I just don't get it. I was home all night, working on my paper on *Slaughterhouse-Five*."

"Did you finish it?"

"Yeah."

"Good book?"

He sounds pleasant all of a sudden, which really throws me off. "Yeah, it's amazing. Every time someone dies in the book, Vonnegut writes, *So it goes*, to heighten the sense of, you know, absurdity. But I made it more difficult for myself by writing it from the point of view of an alien."

"That sounds lame."

I shrug. "So far, I've gotten an A on everything in Bernstein's class. He thinks I should be a writer."

"He's a closet faggot."

"Bernstein?"

"Yeah, Bernstein."

"So?"

"So, nothing. I don't care. I transferred out of there as fast as I could."

"Is something wrong?"

He looks over at me. "No. Why do you always ask that?"

"I've never asked that."

"Yeah. You have. You always think something is wrong."

"You just . . . seem in a bad mood."

"Girls are always so sweet when you first go out, then they get demanding."

The comment is so unfair that I don't even answer. He pulls into his parking space. I can't believe I actually used to watch his stupid space. I get out and walk ahead of him.

"Hey," he calls. "Wait up."

"What?"

"Don't you think a boyfriend and girlfriend should walk into school together?" He puts his arm around me.

"I guess."

"So, whatever happened with that job at CVS?"

"I told you. When I called to reschedule, she said that if I couldn't make the interview, she had others who could." My voice comes out mad.

"Don't get a job. I want you to have time for me. You look so pretty today."

Find a new line, I want to say.

ROGER

EVERY TIME I pick up Sage she gives me a bag of sweets with cute names like "blondies," "raspberry bliss," or "almond crunchies." It's like she expects an engagement ring in return.

Last night, she gave me "cherry dreams." They looked, honest to God, like some squirrel had puked on a baking pan. "You really want to do me a favor?" I said. "Bring me a cheeseburger."

She went quiet then, and spent the whole drive looking out the window like there was something interesting out there rather than trees.

"Just joking," I said. "Can't you take a joke?"

"It wasn't funny." But she let me kiss her after that, so it was okay. But, just kiss.

I'm getting nowhere with her. I should dump her. But she's . . . I don't know. She's a good listener. She's sweeter than most girls. Not a schemer. She doesn't think she's *all that*.

I told her I didn't like her hanging out with the Thespians, that they were weirdos, that it made her look bad and me look bad. I said I needed her to be available.

She got all upset about that, said that she had to run the shows or they wouldn't happen. As soon as she got a job she'd have to quit anyway, she told me.

The other weird thing is she won't let me meet her mom. Not that I really care.

She met my parents a couple of times. My mom said she was sweet. My dad said, "Why do you always pick girls with flat chests?" but it wasn't a question that really expected an answer.

I asked Reenie about her mom. "The mom's certifiable," she said.

"You're kidding."

"Seriously. Sage tries to hide it, but everyone knows it. The mom's . . . crazy. And they're poor as dirt."

"Her mom and the boyfriend lit the curtains on fire."

She thought that was hilarious. "Oh my God. Poor Sage." Then she leaned toward me. I thought she was going to kiss me or something, but she was just brushing something off my shirt. "Crumbs," she said.

The crumbs were from the squirrel puke, which actually tasted pretty good.

"How come you don't have a boyfriend?" I asked.

She looked right at me with those big eyes. "Because you're taken."

I almost asked her out right then and there. I mean, I like Sage. Sage is more natural and wholesome. She's not the type that would ever cheat on a guy. But just to leave my options open, I said, "Maybe I'm taken. Maybe not."

SAGE

MOM'S VISITING hours are from twelve to two o'clock.

I've spent the whole morning reading about bipolar disorder: the manic stage with grandiose thoughts, paranoia, crazy behaviors, insomnia, and rapid speech; the depressive stage with its dead flatness.

All of the things that I think of as Mom—the carelessness with money, the religiousness, the inappropriate flirtations—are part of the disorder.

Then there were testimonials:

"I went from one extreme to another, so that my kids would wonder 'which dad' they were getting. I chased after every woman I saw and spent all the money in our savings account."

"I was sure God spoke to me and me only."

"I talked 24-7. I talked so fast, people couldn't understand my words."

"I loved the highs, but the lows were terrible. I became an invalid."

It's treatable with medication, just like Mrs. G. said. People can lead "normal" lives.

Ⅹ Ⅹ Ⅹ Ⅹ

Driving to the hospital, I remember the time Mom and I went to Six Flags. It was a period where she was trying to be a good mom; like she had a how-to guide on building a bicycle or constructing an outhouse.

We sang on the drive there, songs like "She'll Be Coming 'round the Mountain" and "Oh Susannah." She bought cotton candy and popcorn.

The first ride was called the "haunted house." When we got to the front of the line, we realized the ride was actually a roller coaster.

"Maybe she's too short." Mom pointed to me.

The attendant took his ruler and measured me. "Just makes it. Leave your purse here so it doesn't fly away."

He strapped us into a car. "Do you think he'll steal the money from my purse?" Mom asked me.

"Maybe." As the car chugged up a slope, I worried about what we would do if the boy stole Mom's money.

Then the car plunged and I forgot everything. My neck snapped and my stomach dropped. We swerved right and left, then hung upside down. I was sure we'd be flung to the ground at any moment.

When the ride finally ended, Mom had to help me get off. My legs were noodles. I felt like I was going to hurl.

But Mom was elated. "What fun!" She clapped her hands. "Let's go again!"

That's what it's been. Not an original metaphor, but one that fits the bill.

A roller-coaster life.

And me, scared to death.

XXXX

The hospital looks pretty normal. I expected locked doors and patients in straightjackets, but it looks like most hospitals: long corridors, white walls, overhead lights. There're just twice as many nurses as normal. "The visiting area is being retiled," a nurse tells me, "so you can sit with your mom in her room."

"How's she doing?"

"Fine!" The nurse smiles. "Your mom's really popular."

As I approach the door, I feel shy. Years of mistakes and misunderstandings pool up in my eyes and I stand like a statue, blinking.

"Have a nice visit." The nurse pats my arm. A line from a Tennessee Williams play goes through my mind. "I have always depended on the kindness of strangers."

XXXX

Mom is perched on the end of the bed, watching TV. Across the room, a woman sits in a chair facing the wall. *Oprah* is on, a show about women who lost weight and transformed their lives, women who wanted *to be Mona.*

I sit on the bed. Mom doesn't speak until the commercial. "She gave them all cars." Her voice is flat.

"What?"

"Oprah. One time she gave the audience cars."

"I brought you some raspberry bars." I open the container. The scent of raspberry, oats, and brown sugar drifts up. My mouth waters. I pick one up, then remember Roger saying my jeans looked too tight. I put it back. "Who's that?" I whisper.

Mom glances over at her roommate. "Bernice. She's giving herself time-out. She's almost always in time-out." Mom takes a bite. "These are wonderful. The oats are so crispy."

"Thanks." It's been so long since she noticed anything I baked.

"Bernice! Want a raspberry bar? My daughter is an excellent baker. She's going to be a chef."

The woman in the chair rushes over, grabs one, then returns to her chair.

"Good girl, Bernice." Mom whispers, "She needs a lot of coaxing to come out of her shell." *Oprah* comes back on. Mom's eyes go to the TV.

"Mom. Can we turn off the TV?"

"I'm enjoying it."

"I'm only here for an hour."

She turns off the TV. "I'll miss you when you go."

I try to think of a reply, but my eyes blink and my throat feels like I've swallowed a sock, so I get up and offer another treat to Bernice, who takes two. Mom looks back at the TV as if there's a picture there. "I'm sorry it took me so long to come," I say. "The doctor said to wait."

"The doctor's very nice. He comes to see me each day."

She always has loved attention. "So, Mom, what do you do here, aside from watch TV?"

"I get lots of shots and blood tests. They're very interested in my blood. I take pills. We sit in groups and answer questions. We're supposed to face our feelings, and talk about them, which is . . . painful. There's a meditation class. They gave me a mantra that I'm supposed to use: 'OM.' But I know my real mantra."

"What?"

"'Why couldn't I have made him stay?'"

"Dad?"

"Things were better when he was here. He held everything together. Why couldn't I have made him stay?"

"That's *my* mantra, Mom. You stole my mantra."

"It wasn't your job to make him stay. You were only four."

"I guess we have to move on from that."

"I guess. So how about you?" She finally looks at me. "Are you okay? Do you have enough money to get by?"

"I'm fine."

"What about the bills? I should give you my checkbook and show you how to sign my name, so you can pay them."

"Is there money in the account?"

"I don't know." She looks at the floor. "A check should be coming in."

"A check?"

"I need to get home to take care of these things." She stands up and looks around the room, like she's going to pack up. "I shouldn't be here."

"I can take care of everything. Just tell me what needs to be done."

"I'm ready to go home."

"They want to wait until the medication stabilizes."

"It's *me* that they want to stabilize, not the medication." She begins to cry. "The day your dad left, the roof leaked. Do you remember?"

"You've told me, but I don't remember."

"I had put on the TV and crawled onto the couch. You wanted to watch *Sesame Street* and I wanted to watch *Regis*, so we took turns. It was the day after Christmas. It rained and rained. We didn't leave the couch the whole day. We pretended we were on a boat. Then drip, drip, drip."

"How did it get fixed?"

"I don't remember. No, I do. Miriam called someone. She took us to the mall and fed us lunch, while it was being fixed. You know what she told me the other day? She said the only reason they haven't moved is that they wanted to look out for *us*."

"Embarrassing."

"My life is embarrassing," she says.

"But I read a book about it. Bipolar is a disease. And if you take the medication, you'll be okay. You already seem better. You'll be like . . . normal."

"Normal is boring." She reaches for a tissue and dabs at her eyes.

"Maybe, but what good is it feeling all revved up if no one can share in your reality? If it's not reality to begin with?"

Mom smiles. "I should have named you Star. Because that's what you are to me, the bright light in my life."

"Do you know what today is?"

"I don't even know what month it is."

"It's my birthday!"

"Is it? Oh my God!"

"I'm eighteen."

"Oh, I don't have a present here for you. I'm sorry. Eighteen!" She looks panicked. "Now you can leave me and go on with your life and be happy."

"I won't leave you," I promise.

Then we're both crying and on the boat again, hanging on to the sides so we don't capsize.

VERN

THE SNOW MELTED in one hot day. The world is flooded. I had to carry Sophie across the gutter, so she wouldn't be covered in mud. She decided the synagogue in Providence was too liberal for her tastes. So twice a week, I have to haul her to Boston to Hebrew school. It's not bad when Walter comes, though. Like today, we're hanging out in Brookline at Sumo Sushi, where plates of sushi float by on a canal and you grab what you want.

"I've got to do something about Cassandra." I grab a plate of octopus. "She's so persistent. She can't get it into her brain that *someone* on the planet doesn't want to be with her. Like Saturday; she begged me to go to the island, and I was feeling so bummed, I went. She packed a lunch, disgusting bologna sandwiches with yellow mustard—*yellow*, Walter—warm Cokes, and stale cookies that made me incredibly depressed."

"Why would cookies make you depressed?"

"It's just that . . ." I feel like I'm going to cry. "I've had better."

He grabs a plate of futomaki. "Want some?"

"You're a bottomless pit today."

"I'm in a good mood."

"Why are you in a good mood?"

"I got into Berkeley." Walter gives a rare smile.

"That's awesome! Why didn't you tell me?"

"San Francisco, here I come."

"Man! Dinner's on me."

"It was gonna be on you, anyway."

"Well, on my dad. Congrats."

"Thanks."

"You are destined for greatness."

"I suspect that greatness entails misery, like those singers in the old days who had to cut off their balls in order to preserve their high voices."

"What were they called?"

"Castrati. Besides, my intellect is part of my pathology."

"Thinking you have a pathology is part of your pathology."

"Is that a riddle or a tongue twister? So . . . Cassandra. Bad cookies, bad news. Yellow mustard. What happened next?"

"She tugs me behind this fort on the beach and she goes, 'Let's do it.'"

"How did it feel?"

"How did it feel?"

"Being offered the golden key by Cassandra Parks?"

"Like a glacier. An iceberg. Like I was the *Titanic* hitting an iceberg."

"Too many metaphors! You're gonna blow one of my circuits."

"But . . . an opportunity comes, you know, and I . . . blow it."

"An opportunity?"

"Yeah, to do it, to figure out how to do it."

"To figure out?" He laughs.

"To break in, to learn the ropes."

"Stop while you're ahead."

"Yeah, okay. That's what I did."

"You stopped?" Walter grabs a California roll.

"I said, 'I like to get to know a person a little better before I, you know, *do it*.'"

"Sounding like . . ."

". . . the virgin I am. Okay, yeah. This is torture to even talk about. And don't mention it to anyone because it's, you know, not exactly cool to talk about your sex life even if you don't like the girl."

"Who am I going to tell? My mommy? Try some of this."

"Talking about this makes me lose my appetite."

"But you're still taking Cassandra to the prom. Right?"

"Yeah, I'm so excited I think I'll move to Afghanistan."

"You know what your problem is?"

"What?"

"You love another."

"That's it?"

"It may sound old-fashioned, but sexual excitement does tend to accompany emotional attachments like love, or at least *like*. It would be like Roger Willis presenting his bare butt to me. Know what I would do . . . ?"

"Do we have to talk about Roger? That is a nauseating image."

"I would hurl. Because I hate the bastard. Like you say . . . nauseating. And you are pretty much using Cassandra as a substitute for Sage. Bad cookies for good cookies. Now if someone I was attracted to presented his—"

"I get the point, Walter. Let's not go there."

"You don't accept me?"

"I accept you. Okay? We're here. We're friends. I just don't think we need details about male-to-male relationships. That does not turn my crank."

"Yeah, you're my best friend. You kept me from hanging myself with Twizzlers. Remember?"

"The Twizzlers wouldn't have held your weight. Not the way you had them knotted. And the basketball hoop would've broken. It's not like I rescued you from a burning building."

"You saved me when I was getting beat up."

"I tripped the breaker. I'm a regular Messiah."

"So . . ."

"So forget about it."

"Sage'll come around. She will."

"It's not right. Me with Cassandra. Sage with Roger. It's like black and white making red."

"Or fuchsia, a much more interesting color."

"Just do me a favor."

"Sure."

"Look out for Sage. Because she hasn't come near me since that creep arrived, and I have my hands full with Cassandra. You watch out for Sage."

"Will do. I'll watch her like a hawk. I won't let you down."

I QUIT as stage manager for *Grease*. "You can't do this to me," Madame Thespian cried. "The production will die without you."

"I have to get a job," I explained. "And I'm getting behind on my homework." I left off the part about Roger insisting I quit and calling her 'Madame Lesbian.'

"You're a flake." She dismissed me with a wave of her hand. Four years of my hard work erased.

To make matters worse, Bernstein has us writing plays with characters from the books. He paired us up and guess who my partner is? Mona Simms.

"Do you want to work at my house or your house?" she said.

"Let's just do our parts separately, then we can cut and paste them," I said.

"But . . . we're supposed to work together. Like, in one room."

"I'm busy." It came out rudely.

It was weird. Tears started sliding down her face onto the desk.

That freaked me right out. "Don't stress. We'll get together. Let's go to Happy Diegos."

"It closed." She wiped her eyes.

"Happy Diegos?"

"Yeah. Isn't that sad? My dad and I used to go there sometimes. They're already putting in another restaurant."

Happy Diegos is where Vern and I hung out all the time. Now it's closed, like our friendship. "I'll come to your house, then."

She smiled. I guess she likes getting her way.

✗ ✗ ✗ ✗

Now I'm driving down Mona's long driveway. The house is huge and gorgeous, white with black shutters. A maid answers the door, like in a movie.

"Hi." Mona bounces down the stairs. "Hungry?"

"No."

"Thirsty? Want a Coke?"

"I'm okay."

"Sorry about earlier. I feel so dumb."

"It's okay. With cheerleading and being president and all, you must be pretty stressed."

"It's just . . . I know it's lame . . . but I can't stand it when someone doesn't like me." She looks down. "It, like, hurts my feelings. My dad always tells me I should get thicker skin, but this is the skin I have."

I only wanted to be you. "I-I like you."

"You don't have to. God, I remember in third and fourth grades, inviting you to my birthday parties, and you never came."

"You invited me to your birthday party?"

"Yeah. You don't remember? We were in the same class."

Mom! "I remember being in class with you, and you having a birthday party and everything. I just don't remember being invited."

"I asked you both years. And I invited you over to my house once too."

"My mom was really bad about keeping track of stuff like that."

"I'm just getting all nostalgic. I mean, life as we know it is coming to an end."

"Yeah." *For some of us, that's a good thing*, I want to tell her. "Your house is nice. It's so huge. Do you have brothers and sisters?"

"When my parents bought this house; the plan was to fill it with kids. But they ended up getting divorced and now my mom lives in Florida. So it's just me and my dad. And Maria." She gestures toward the house-keeper. "She's been with us since I was four."

"Do you ever see your mom?"

"In the summer. She lives in Palm Beach. But I hate it. It's a giant sauna and there are huge insects. She doesn't really want me there. It sucks." Her eyes go all watery. "My way of dealing is to stay busy. Do you want to sit outside? It's so nice out."

"Sure." I follow her through the beautiful kitchen to the deck, which looks out over the ocean. Of course. If I lived here I would never go anywhere, not even Palm Beach.

"What should we write about?"

I pull out my notes. "I thought we might do a dialogue between Billy Pilgrim and Buddha, like if they meet up in some intergalactic café."

"Brilliant. I knew I was lucky to work with you." Her smile is so sincere that it's hard not to like her.

We take turns writing a line. All these years, Mona has been the focus of my envy and desire, and she's just a nice, normal person. Rich, yes. Beautiful, yes. But, normal. A person I could've been friends with, if I'd been less intimidated, like Walter, who's just started hanging around with me. He's so funny and smart. I hate to admit it, but I stayed away from him partly because he was so unpopular.

Maria brings iced tea and lemon cookies. I nibble the corner of one, promising myself to eat only half. The iced tea is sprigged with mint. Yeah, I don't need to *be* Mona, but I wouldn't mind having her life!

"Wow, it's five o'clock," Mona says. "Time flies. My dad's taking me to look for a prom dress at six. It's so funny when he goes out shopping with me. He'll be looking through the racks for my size with the moms. 'Do you like this?' 'Do you like this?' He gets a lot of attention."

"Who are you going to the prom with?"

"I don't know. A bunch of guys asked me, so I have to decide really soon."

"Who?"

"Al Smith, George Parkins, Sam Browning, Roger Willis—he always asks—Marty Goldsmith . . ."

She keeps naming names, but I'm not listening. *Roger asked her to the prom? Maybe that's why he hasn't asked me.*

"The problem is," she goes on, "the one person I like hasn't asked me."

"Roger Willis asked you?" My voice comes out shaky.

She covers her mouth. "Oh! Foot in mouth. You're going out with him, aren't you?"

All of my good feelings for her evaporate. "Not for that long," I manage to say.

"I'm sure when he asked me it was *before* that. Like a long, long time ago. Fall." She doesn't sound truthful, but I want to believe her.

"Did you used to go out with him?" *I mean, your picture was on his dash.*

"No! Never. He's too . . ."

"What?"

"Nothing." She picks up the pitcher of iced tea and refills my glass.

I wait for my heart to stop pounding and for my face to cool down. "So, who is it you like?"

"You won't tell? Because he's going out with my friend so I really shouldn't like him."

"Cross my heart."

"Vern Goldburg."

"Vern?"

"I never noticed him that much before the election. But he was such a good sport about it. He is so funny and smart and *himself*. I mean, he's got a nerdy quality too, but he's also got, like, class. Most of the boys our age don't. They think that going out on a date means groping you the whole night. Know what I mean?"

"Yeah."

"But he's with Cassie, so what can I do?"

Mona likes Vern. My stomach twists even tighter. "Vern's a great guy. He lives next door to me."

"Really? Well, do me a favor. If he ever breaks up with Cassie, let me know."

"Okay," I lie.

She touches my hand. "As for Roger?"

"What?"

I can tell she's trying to decide something. "Just . . . be careful."

WAL-MART

THE FIRST TIME I set foot in a Wal-Mart, I was thirteen years old. Since my dad died, money had gotten tighter and tighter, so my mom decided to economize.

The lack of air and light in the store reminded me of what it would feel like to be a coal miner trapped in a shaft.

An old lady with one leg hobbled up to us on crutches. She wore a royal blue vest, a sickening color.

At that time I didn't know the facts of the place: that Wal-Mart was run by a right-wing, "family values" type, that they shorted people their break time, paid low wages, and gave employees hours that left them just short of getting benefits. I didn't know that their treatment of the workforce had lowered standards nationwide.

Still, I could intuit something nasty. Bad vibes.

We walked through the aisles to the boys' clothing. My mom held up various articles, everything navy blue or gray. I hate both of those colors. They're barely even colors. Oh yes, there was a third "color": camouflage. Very popular in the US of A.

I folded my arms and refused everything. She got upset and I felt guilty. Same ol', same ol'.

When we got into the car, I started crying.

My mom practically drove off the road. "What's the matter?"

"Why did you name me Walter?"

"It's a fine name."

"Walter Martin! Walter Martin!"

"It's not only nice, it's normal."

"What store were we just in?"

"Wal-Mart. Why?" She got a startled look. "Oh. Oh, dear. Well, nobody—"

"*Everybody* calls me that. Everybody. For years."

"I've never heard Vern call you that."

"Vern is the reincarnation of Gandhi. And it's a cheap-shit store."

"Don't talk like that. How long has this been going on?"

"Like, since second grade."

"Oh, Walter, I'm sorry. I'm so, so sorry. You were named after your grandfather. He was a doctor at Johns Hopkins. He wasn't a discount store. He had dignity."

"It doesn't matter."

"Well, we won't go there ever again."

"Great."

"I can never do anything right. I've devoted my life to you. I don't date or work so that I'll be available to you when you need me."

"Sorry I mentioned it."

"We can change your name. What name do you want? I'll go to the town hall and get it changed. George is a nice name. So is Elvis. I'll bet there's no one in this town named Elvis. Pick a new name; any name."

"Matthew Shepard," I said, to be mean.

But she didn't remember the college kid who was beaten, hung up on a fence, and left for dead because he was gay.

She didn't know that gay teens are four times as likely to kill themselves as straight teens.

She'll watch *Queer Eye for the Straight Guy*, or *The Ellen DeGeneres Show* and say, "I think it's so brave when those gays come out in public."

Come out? I didn't even have the choice. I've had the voice, the gestures, since I was two. I was being called faggot before I even knew what the word meant.

"Matthew. I like it. It's New Testament—but why change your last name?"

I didn't answer. When I went home I got some hangers and foil and I fashioned myself a pair of antennae, then sat in front of the TV. "This will be a test," I said. "For the next sixty seconds we will be testing the emergency broadcast system. In the event of a real emergency this system would instruct you on where to go and how to proceed. If a nuclear bomb is dropped, hide under your desk. If there's a tornado, bring your dog, Toto. If you fall down a hole, ignore the rabbits. If terrorists attack, make up a war. A bird in the hand is worth one in the pie. You made your bed, now lie in it. When life gives you lemons, hide."

✗ ✗ ✗ ✗

The next day, I was dragged to my first shrink.

SAGE

I HAVE THE WORST COLD. Mom has one too. When I talked to her this morning on the phone, I could barely make out what she was saying, her voice was so raspy. She asked me about school and if I had enough groceries and such. I lied and said everything was fine. It is so weird having her act normal; flat, but normal.

The mirror is pretty horrifying. My nose belongs to Rudolph the reindeer. My eyes are puffy and I'm mouth breathing, which gives me a slightly retarded look.

This *would* happen on the night Roger is taking me to a party with his friends.

I hear Vern's car drive up, the doors open and close, voices. I resist the urge to look out the window.

I do that sometimes. Watch the whole family. I can see them eating dinner from the kitchen window. For as long as I can remember, I was in and out of their house like it was mine. Now I'm an outsider. My own fault.

The sound of Roger's truck follows. He's on time the one time I'm running late.

I turn off all the lights but one. I just opened the

electric bill; it's a hundred and eight dollars. That check Mom told me would be coming hasn't arrived yet. Her bank account has a hundred dollars. I'm eight shy of electric, although the food stamps arrived, so at least I can eat in the dark.

X X X X

As soon as I climb into the truck, Roger drives off; he doesn't even wait for me to put on my seat belt.

Usually, I try to make conversation, but my throat is scratchy and my head achy, so I just close my eyes.

"I heard you were at Mona's house," he finally says.

"Yeah. We had a project for Bernstein's class."

"You didn't mention it."

No, because whenever I get together with people, you act like I've committed a crime. "It was a dialogue between the characters in different books. Mona wrote one part and I wrote the other. It turned out to be pretty funny. The hypothetical questions are back in Bernstein's class. I'd kind of missed them. They get everyone talking."

"The point is?" he says.

"N-nothing."

"What's with your voice?" His phone rings. I can tell it's one of his football buddies, because he gets loud and uses obscenities.

I should feel happy. I'm going to a party. Mom's better. A miracle. So what's wrong with me?

"See you soon, loser!" He hangs up the phone.

"Al?"

"Yeah. So . . . did you have fun at Mona's? I mean . . . did she say anything *interesting*?"

"Not really." *Just that you asked her to the prom, when you haven't asked me.*

"Don't talk to her. She can't be trusted."

"Trusted how?"

"She's a phony, that's all. One of your best traits is that you're *not* friends with Mona."

Is that a trait? "Did you used to go out with her or something?"

His phone rings yet again. The timing on that thing is uncanny. "Hello. We're here. Shut up."

There's a dilapidated ranch house. Kids are pouring out the front door, hanging on the lawn, which is already covered in beer cans and bottles. When we get out of the car, he walks ahead of me.

As soon as we enter, Al rushes over. "Dude, you've got to see this."

"Be right back." Roger plants a kiss on my cheek and disappears into the crowded room.

I look around. It's loud and people keep bumping

into me so that I feel like I'm invisible and a giant, both. It would be so nice to be home with Selfish on the couch, or better yet, playing Balderdash with Sophie and Vern. My brain is pounding. I head for the kitchen to find a drink.

"Who're you?" a guy asks, when I grab a Coke.

The guy looks about thirty, although he's dressed like a teenager: long hair flopped over a bald spot, a Hawaiian shirt with a leather necklace, torn jeans.

"I came with Roger. Is this your house?"

"Yeah. So you're Roger's babe. That's cool. He didn't tell me you were such a babe."

"Nice house," I say, although it's small and dark and smells like stale beer and smoke and maybe pee.

"It does for a crib. Wanna see my bedroom?"

Life versus fantasy. The fantasy: a party thrown by Rachael Ray, ten or twelve people munching on appetizers listening to Dave Matthews, Roger by my side.

"No, thanks. I'd better go find Roger."

The fantasy: that I could be Mona. Thin and with a popular boyfriend, I'm still me, looking for my place in the world. I head out the other side of the kitchen.

"If you don't find him, come back and find me, babe."

I shove through the bodies. If I keep moving, no one will notice I'm alone.

"Dudette!" A guy stumbles into me. "Let's go dance."

I push past him and see a welcome sight. Fern, Reenie, and Caroline are sitting on the floor in a corner. I am so relieved to find friends.

"Hi!" I plop down.

"So Roger finally brought you to one of Abe's parties," Caroline says.

Finally?

"Where's Roger?" Reenie says. "Is he here?"

Why does she care? "Yeah."

"Want a hit?" Fern passes me a joint.

"I have a cold."

"It'll cure it and give you good dreams."

"Last night," Caroline says, "I dreamed I was a pelican and my jaw was full of fish. I was flying over some, like, starving people, dropping them fish."

"That's so phallic." Fern laughs.

"Nuh-uh!" Caroline says. "What is . . . phallic?"

"I'll bet *you* dream about Roger every night," Reenie says.

"Not really." *What is her problem?*

"Why should she dream it, when she has the reality," Fern says; I get the feeling she's defending me.

"No reason." Reenie stands up. "I'm going for a

beer. I'd bring one to you, but I'm not coming back." She disappears into the crowd.

"Skank," Caroline says, then she gets up and follows her.

"I've got my own supplies." Fern opens her purse and pulls out two tiny bottles. "Fly the friendly skies." She hands me one. "Reenie is really jealous of you."

"Me?" I take a swig. It tastes foul, although it makes my throat less scratchy. I finish the bottle.

"You like that, huh?" Fern jokes. "Maybe you're a vodka girl." She pulls out a couple more.

The vodka goes down smoother; it barely has any taste at all. I don't admit to her that the only alcohol I've ever tasted is beer and wine. "What are you, like, going on airplanes all the time?"

"My dad's a pilot, so yeah."

"Really?"

"Yeah, and my mom was a stewardess. Isn't that too damn cute?" She hands me another vodka.

"Wow, I think this cured my cold."

"It'll make you forget your cold, anyway."

I glance around the room. "I wonder if Roger's looking for me."

"Good catch, huh?" Fern says.

"Roger?"

"Yeah. Mr. Popularity Hunk. Fifteen minutes of fame. Right?"

"Uh . . ." Around me, the room is loosening. "Is Mona here?"

"Mona Simms? No. She's too much of a goody-goody to come to one of these. I've never met anyone more uptight."

"Oh?"

"To relaxation." She hands me another bottle. "Four's a charm."

I start to get why people drink; it's like an eraser is moving across my brain, wiping out my obsessive worries. "A foreign concept."

"Huh?"

"Relaxation. That's foreign to me."

"That's a good one."

"Why do you think Reenie's jealous of me?"

"Because you have Roger. Because you're one of the few kids who doesn't pretend to be someone else, and everyone likes you."

"You're kidding?"

"No." Fern has long red hair, a necklace made of seaweed, a man's shirt, and seashell earrings and bracelet. She's definitely herself. "Reenie's, like, lost. That's my analysis of the situation, anyway."

"Analysis." That phrase puts me into hysterics. Fern laughs with me, but then she stops. "Uh-oh. Here comes trouble."

Roger storms over, practically tripping on me. "Let's go."

"I'm having fun."

"I just kinda got into a fight."

"With who?" Fern says. "I want to watch."

"None of your business."

"I'll bet it was Cor-butt. You always pick fights with Cor-butt."

Why does everyone know so much about Roger, except me?

Roger pulls me up by the arm.

"Ow." I try to say good-bye to Fern, but I feel so wasted all of a sudden, I'm afraid that my words will come out backward.

X X X X

The night air is like a slap on my face.

Roger opens the door and jumps into the driver's side. For a minute I think he's going to drive off without me. "What are you waiting for, Sage? Let's go."

I climb in. "The party was warm, but your truck is cold."

"How much did you drink? I only left you for, like, ten minutes."

"It was an hour." It comes out angry. "I thought we were going to the party *together*."

"Are you going to pick a fight with me? I hope not. Because I am in a very bad mood."

"What happened?"

"Oh, it's just some bullshit from last year when I, like, borrowed a couple hundred bucks from Corbett and he keeps insisting I didn't pay him back."

"Did you?"

"Yeah. I paid him. At least, I thought I did. Maybe I didn't. But I said I did, and he should believe me."

He's driving faster than usual, or maybe it's just my stomach and brain. They feel like they're dangling at the back of the truck, like those tin cans on fishing wire: JUST MARRIED.

"I'd prefer it if you don't hang out with Fern."

"Fern, too?"

"She's into drugs, in case you didn't notice."

"She's the only person at the school who doesn't act like everyone else."

"That's because she's *not* like everyone else."

"I don't want you hanging out with Al Smith," I taunt.

"Don't be ridiculous. He's my best friend."

"I thought I was your best friend."

"You're my *girl*friend."

"Same thing."

"No. It's not."

"Where are we going?"

"The park. I thought we could, you know, park."

"Maybe I should go home. I don't feel well. I think I breathed in some of that pot."

"You breathed in alcohol. I didn't think you were that type. We'll get you sober before you go home."

"It doesn't matter."

"What's your mom going to say if I bring you home drunk?"

Nothing. She's locked up. "She'll be asleep. I want to go home."

He turns into the park, drives up the hill. I remember how good I felt that day I ran past here, like I was in charge of my life. For once.

"Sorry I left you alone at the party." He turns off the ignition. "I didn't mean to. I was just going to get us drinks."

"The drinks were in the kitchen. You went in the other direction."

"You're so pretty." He kisses me.

My lips are numb and my stomach is roiling, but I try to kiss him back.

"I can taste everything you drank tonight." He's on

top of me, pressing on me, his hands everywhere, like he's trying to disassemble me. "Vodka, tequila. Baby, you are so sexy."

That's a new one. "I thought I was pretty."

"We've been going out three months. I've been really patient."

"I'm not ready."

"We don't have to go all the way. Just . . . try something for me. All the girls do it." He keeps pushing and pulling me and he's talking about Mona at the same time, or maybe I'm just thinking about her, that I felt somehow safe with her.

"Stop it!" I shove him hard.

"Do what I say!" He pulls me back toward him.

That is the key to our relationship, I realize; that I do what he says. He pushes my head toward his lap. "Just do this one thing for me."

"I said no!" I jerk up. My head connects with his face. "Ow! Shit!"

I spring back to my side of the truck, then fumble with the door.

But he grabs my arm and squeezes so hard, it feels like it will snap: my bones, my paper skin, my heart will snap.

ROGER

SO I TWISTED HER ARM A LITTLE. B.F.D. We were parked like we always do. I could tell she was wasted because she was trying so hard to act like she wasn't. This was going to be our last date if she didn't put out, because who needs that. Who needs it when there're about twenty other girls who are willing?

I told her that if she went down on me it really wasn't sex, it was just, like, doing me a favor, 'cause I like her so much and she turns me on. I go, "You won't get pregnant or anything. That's the beauty of it."

Then, I don't know why I said this, but all of a sudden it just popped out of my mouth. 'Mona went down on me! If it's good enough for her, why not you?'"

She jumped back, like I hit her. It was weird. Like, why should she care what Mona did? "She did not." Her words were totally slurred.

"Yeah. She did."

"She can't stand you," Sage said.

"What did Mona tell you?" I was so pissed. Because Mona, the bitch, could never give me the time of the day. Mona and her lawyer dad called the police and put a restraining order on me just because I was a little persistent. They almost got me kicked off the football team.

I was just coaxing a little when I pushed Sage's head down, but then she was so drunk that she jerked her head up right into my face. It was like being tackled on the football field, pain bringing out the worst in me, which works in football but not with a girl.

She tried to get out of the car. No way was I letting her wander around drunk. I was drunk too, I guess. A little. Five beers. I grabbed her too hard. You got to excuse a guy if he's drunk.

Then, all of a sudden, someone was banging on the window. Like a cop. A damn army sergeant.

It was that faggot, Wal-Mart. He was wearing a trench coat. There could be anything under that coat, I thought. A knife. A gun.

Sage rolled down the window. She was sober enough to do that.

"Hey, guys," Wal-Mart said. "I thought this was your truck." Like he's my buddy or something.

Sage, as soon as she saw him, started crying. Wal-Mart looked past her at me. If his eyes were guns they would've been firing bullets.

"Get lost, faggot," I said. "Can't you see we're on a date?"

"But your date is crying." Bullet eyes.

"She's just drunk. Aren't you, Sage?"

"Maybe she wants me to take her home," he said.

"Maybe she wants me to break your nose."

"I can take you out," Wal-Mart said. "I can and I will."

Freshman and sophomore year, I had this kid groveling on the ground; he was so scared of me. But something about the way he looked at me. I let go of her arm.

Sage opened the door, jumped out, and slammed the door behind her.

By the time I got out of the car, they were running down the hill toward the street.

✗ ✗ ✗ ✗

Later, I drove past her house. The lights were on, but her crazy mom's car was in the driveway, so I couldn't call.

I even got out and went up to the door. I figured if the mom was asleep I could sneak in and patch things up. But a light was on, and I remembered the mom's boyfriend. What if Sage told them and they were up?

I saw something move, like a snake, in an empty planter by the door. God, it startled me.

It was the cat, the one she always goes on about, a freaky, scraggly black cat. I thought, *Fine. You want to run out on me. Let's see how much fun it is to wake up to find your cat with a broken neck.* As decrepit as the thing looked, I'd be doing it a favor.

I reached toward it, but it arched its back like some kind of Halloween spook and hissed. I thought, *What I want is to make up with her. Screwing with her cat is not the point.* I tried to pet it, a sort of apology for my angry thoughts, but the little fucker just snarled, scratched my hand, and ran off.

So I sat in my truck all night, watching her window, thinking: *Already, she's missing me.*

SAGE

THE NIGHT OF THE ROGER FIASCO, Walter was so sweet. He took me home, then held my hair back while I puked into the toilet. "God, I can't believe I was with him," I kept saying. "It's like someone just threw a bucket of cold water on me and brought me to my senses."

"That would be me. And for the record, I can't believe you were with him either. You must've thought he was someone else."

"Exactly."

"Willis is one of those guys who thinks that being a man is bullying a woman."

"Yeah."

"Or a gay."

"Walter, I'm sorry."

"Why?"

"That I haven't gotten to know you all these years."

"Well, I didn't exactly invite you over for tea."

"Thank you."

"Anything for . . ."

"For?"

"For a friend," he said.

So now I'm Roger-less.

It's strange. To not be waiting by the phone (although it keeps ringing), or for him to drive up, to not be worrying that I'm going to say or do something wrong all the time.

I thought I would miss him, but all I feel is relieved.

The one I miss is Vern. I screwed up. Big time. Treated him like he was something to wipe off my shoes. That's what's killing me right now.

At least the social worker came by. "While your mom is considered disabled, the state can pay you to look after her," she said.

"Really?"

"It's just a little, but it might help." She looked around the house. My books and papers were spread all over the coffee table. Unfolded laundry was piled up in a corner of the couch. I have to admit, I haven't cleaned anything for weeks.

"Pretty bad, huh?" I said.

"I've seen much worse. At least you *have* a house!"

That made me think. Point of view, like Bernstein says. There are people worse off than me. I have to remember that and be grateful, rather than always compare myself to the well-off kids at school. I have to stop being such a whiner.

"Between us, the financials are tricky," she said. "Your mom's medications are expensive. If she gets a job and earns too much, she could lose her benefits, including medical. So she can only accept a job with health insurance. Don't tell anyone I told you this."

"I won't."

"I encouraged your mom to go back to school. She's a bright lady. If she stays on her meds and focuses . . ."

"Mom? Go to school?"

"She told me she'd like to be a social worker." She smiles. "Like me. Or maybe a nurse."

The phone kept ringing while she was there. "You can answer it," she said. "I don't mind."

"It's just some guy," I explained. "He's mad about our breakup. If someone else calls, they'll leave a message and I'll call them back."

She freaked out about that. "He shouldn't be calling over and over like that. That's abusive." She told me I should call the police and gave me a pamphlet on domestic violence.

I didn't mention him driving back and forth past the house. "I'll just take it off the hook."

She shook her head. "Sometimes, if you've had an erratic parent, you choose an erratic boyfriend."

"Tell me about it." That was Roger. Mr. Confusing.

"Mrs. Goldburg said you could stay with her. Why don't you?"

"I'll be all right."

"Well, you're eighteen. I can't make you do anything." She looked worried.

"If there's a problem, I'll go over to the Goldburgs," I told her. She stood up and gave me her card. "The doctor says your mom will be able to come home soon. She'll switch to outpatient therapy then, so she'll still be monitored. The key is the medication. Whatever you do, don't trust her to take it herself. Watch her put the pill in her mouth and swallow. Once they feel better, patients often think they don't need their meds. A catastrophe. Call me if you need me."

"Thank you."

After she left, I felt lonely. I called Mom, but she was in her group therapy. Then I tried Walter, but he was out with Vern. I could've been with them, if only . . .

That's what Mom has had. A life of "if onlys."

I do not want to live like that.

WAL-MART

I **CAME OUT TO MY MOM.** It was so easy.

We were sitting at dinner. Mom kept wiping her eyes the way she does to provoke maximum guilt feelings.

"What?" I finally said.

"I'm sorry, Walter. It's just . . . in the fall you'll be going away to college. These are our last dinners at home."

"I'll be back for the summer."

"You won't be back. I know it. You'll love Berkeley and San Francisco and you won't come back. You hate it here."

I didn't know she knew that!

"Mom," I said. "I'm gay."

"Yes, yes, Walter," she said impatiently. "I know. You don't have to go on about it."

I was in shock.

"What if . . ." She started clearing the table.

What if we give you ten more years of therapy? Hormone injections? A sex-change operation? "What, Mom?"

She gave me her best Midwestern smile. "What if I

visit you? Would that be too intrusive? California has always seemed so . . . exciting and warm. It would be nice to escape next winter."

All of a sudden, I liked her again. She's felt like this heavy weight all these years, with her hot meals and worry, but the weight was an anchor, too.

"Of course you're coming to visit. Parents' week is in October, for starters. Be there or be square."

Tears and smiles at once. "Honestly, Walter, you say the oddest things."

SAGE

NINE O'CLOCK and I've already run (making sure Roger wasn't out there first), cleaned the kitchen, and started some brownies baking. My plan is to give them to Vern. A peace offering.

Now I'm approaching the dark zone—Mom's room. I avoid it whenever possible. As I walk in, I realize why. The curtains are drawn. The smell of cigarette smoke and mold. Dead air.

I open the door slowly, but no monster pops out. Only chaos: piles of clothes on the floor, dirty cups and plates used as ashtrays, empty cans and wrappers.

I pull the curtains open. Dust flies off, so I yank them down and throw them in the hall. I open the windows, turn on all of the lights, strip the sheets, and toss the laundry on top of the curtains.

x x x x

On the mirrored sliding doors of the closet, she has cut out pages from magazines, faces of models and actresses where her face would be. There's Demi Moore, Kate Winslet, and Meryl Streep. I'm about three inches taller than Mom. My eyes peer out above the faces. Eerie.

I open the doors. Since most of her clothes are on the floor, her closet is practically empty. But in the back are my dad's old suits that she's kept.

I pull them out and lay them on the bed. Once he was here, wearing them, going to work. I remember, all of a sudden, him bringing home cupcakes for me, from the bakery, and him carrying me on his shoulders. It knocks the breath out of me.

The suits smell damp and musty. On the lapels, in neat rows, are burn holes. Someone has taken a cigarette to the suits. It had to be Mom.

I sit on the bed. Dizzy. When did she do that? Was it when he still lived here? Or after he left? What *did* Mom do to make him go? Why did he leave me behind?

My eyes smart. My energy dies. I want to take a nap all of a sudden, but I have to *keep going.*

I'm catching on. This is how to survive, maybe even succeed. *Keep going.* Whether you feel like it or not.

I put the suits back in the closet. On the floor there is a laundry bin full of mail. I take it to the bed and go through it.

It's mostly junk: subscriptions, advertisements, credit card applications (who would give Mom a credit card?).

Then I come to three unopened letters. They're all addressed to my mom at a P.O. box, not here. The name in the left corner is my own name: PRIESTLY, just that, as if I had sent it to myself.

I rip the first envelope open. It's a check for eighteen hundred dollars, signed *Robert Priestly*. The address on the check is a P.O. box in Austin, Texas. No phone number. The check in my hand is a dead thing, a scrap, but what it represents is not. Groceries in the fridge. A person. A place. A life.

Time stops. A breeze sweeps in through the window, stirring up dust, making me sneeze.

In cleaning my mother's room, I have found my father. Literally. Found. Him.

The other envelopes are the same, with checks for November and December. No checks for January or February. That's when Mom got dressed up as Mrs. G., and we had food in the house. She must have cashed those checks, but why not these? Did she just forget?

A check should be coming, Mom said in the hospital. When was she going to tell me that the check doesn't come here, but to a P.O. box I know nothing about?

Rage moves through my blood like a virus. All these years, I wondered how she got by with her part-time jobs. I thought he'd forgotten me completely, but he remembered enough to take out a pen and sign a check the first of every month like clockwork.

And the presents, the ones I've received every birthday and Christmas? It always seemed so odd that Mom could pull together lovely gifts, when the rest of the year, she couldn't even remember to buy Band-Aids. There was the Lite Brite when I was seven, the American Girl dolls with their costumes, the Razor scooter, the laptop and printer when I was fourteen. They had to have been from him.

And she pretended they were from her. Maybe he's even sent letters or cards to me. There could be one there right now for my eighteenth birthday.

Selfish climbs onto my lap, purrs, rubs himself against me. *He* was a gift from my dad when I was three, a little black kitten tucked into a box with a bow on Christmas.

I pick him up and hug him close. He's what's left of my dad.

VERN

COLLEGE ACCEPTANCES COMING IN: University of Vermont, University of New Hampshire, Boston University. My mom holds the letters up to the light and carries on until I open them, then she jumps up and down like it's her who's heading off for the great life adventure.

Interrupting her fervor is a knock on the door. I only know one person who knocks like that, shy, as if she expects to be told to go away, instead of invited in. My heart goes to my throat. All week, Walter has been trying to talk me into going over, but there's just no way. I have *some* pride. "Answer it, Vern," Mom says.

"You answer, Sophie," I say.

"I'm doing my homework." Sophie usually runs for the door.

"Go on," Mom whispers. "I think it's Sage."

"I know who it is," I hiss. *God, it's annoying to have a mom and sister who are so nosy and involved.*

By the time I get to the door, she's gone.

There's just a box there, wrapped in red Christmas paper, my name on it in lettering cut from gold tinsel.

I can already smell the brownies, can feel their warmth in the box. My mouth waters.

First, I eat one. Then I jump over the hedge and go through the kitchen door. Sage is on her knees in the bathroom cleaning the toilet. Did you know it's really hard to be mad at someone cleaning a toilet?

When she sees me she stands up, holding the toilet brush. It's like something from a movie, a comedy.

"I hope you started that *after* you made the brownies."

"I did." Her voice is squeaky, then she starts to cry.

✗ ✗ ✗ ✗

After we finish cleaning, we go out to look for some-place to eat, stopping by to peek into what used to be Happy Diegos.

The door is open at the new restaurant.

"*Le Chat*." Sage reads the sign. "French?"

"At least it's not a chain. Look, someone's there." We wander in.

The inside has only eight tables, each one with a different tablecloth. A guy with a goatee is look-ing around. He notices us. "Which tablecloth do you like?"

"I like the red ones." Sage says. "They make the place look warm. The white ones are too formal.

This isn't a formal kind of town. Actually, you could alternate the red and the gold. That would look nice."

"I never thought of that." He has a French accent. He's . . . Let's put it this way: I could fix him up with Walter.

"Are you the owner?" Sage asks.

"*Oui.*"

"When will you open?" I say.

"Twenty days and one hour. So much to do. I spend hours just deciding the tablecloth."

"Can I have a job?" Sage is totally bold. It is not like her. "I want to be a chef, so I really need experience working in a kitchen."

"Kitchen?"

"I could chop vegetables or something."

"What I need is waitress. Are you eighteen? You have to be eighteen to serve wine."

"Yes, but I've never waitressed."

"I will train you. I need dependable. Thursday through Sunday nights. Piece of cake. Do you have nice clothes? A black dress would be good to wear, or do you think red, like the tablecloth?"

"Black . . . or maybe pink."

"*D'accord.* You start training tomorrow. You need to

know all the foods I serve. Life works like this. I need waitress. *Voilà*. Here you are."

When we get to the car Sage jumps up and down. "You're a good luck charm, Vern." She puts her arms around me and hugs me so tight, I melt like chocolate.

SAGE

DRIVING TO THE HOSPITAL, I keep flashing on that film we watched in Current Events. It was about two poor kids in Iran who have to share one pair of shoes. The sister runs home from morning school and the brother slides into the shoes and dashes to afternoon school, reminding me of my life, of scrambling to hold things together.

After two weeks of stalking me, Roger got bored. I turned a corner one morning at school and Roger had his arms around Reenie. It was too late to turn back, so I passed them, looking the other direction, feeling sick to my stomach.

But it wasn't jealousy. It was concern for Reenie, who is like a kite that gets blown by the wind. God only knows where it will land. And I wanted to say to her what Mona said to me: *Be careful.*

✗ ✗ ✗

I pull into the parking lot of the hospital. Today's my last visit. Next week, Mom'll be home. It's a big day in another way too. I registered for classes at the community college this morning.

"Hello, Sage," the nurse calls. "What goodies have you brought today?"

"Cheese puffs. Try one."

"Maybe just one. You going to have your own bakery someday?"

"Or restaurant, I hope."

"Eve is outside." She mimes smoking and points to the courtyard.

I've become attached to this place, the roaming characters who seem oddly comfortable with themselves, the chatting nurses. Mom likes it here too. It's like she has a life. I'm worried she'll be lonely when she comes home.

She's sitting on the edge of the planter, talking to a woman in a wheelchair. When she sees me, she pats the woman's shoulder and comes over. "Hi, sweetie."

"Hi." I offer my gifts. "I brought you some cheese puffs. Here are your cigarettes."

"Oh, thank God. I just finished my last one." She ignores the cheese puffs, opens the cigarettes and lights up.

I try to feel friendly, but the pool of anger I've been carrying around wells up into my throat. I pop a cheese puff in my mouth and swallow it. "I got a job."

"Did you?" She smiles. "Where?"

"A new French restaurant in Parker's Plaza. I'm a waitress. The owner is very . . . excitable, but he's nice. He's made me taste all the food. It's incredible."

"Is it expensive?"

"Yeah."

"You'll make good tips, then."

"I'm hoping. He's paying me minimum wage for training, so I already got one paycheck."

"Amazing."

"I registered for classes at CCRI for fall, and I'm sending in an application to Johnson & Wales for next winter. My teacher wrote a really nice letter for me."

"Which teacher?"

"Bernstein."

She looks down. "When you were little, I always knew your teachers."

"Yeah." I try to think of more small talk, but then it just blurts out. "Mom, why didn't you cash them?"

"What?"

"I cleaned your room."

"My room?" Mom looks startled.

"I didn't know you had a P.O. box. There were checks from Dad. We were practically starving this winter. Why didn't you cash them?" What I really want to ask is, *Why didn't you tell me about him sending us money?*

She walks over to a bench and sinks into it, like a boxer reeling from a hit.

I sit beside her. "I'm not mad."

"You are. You should be."

"I just don't get it."

"I wanted him to know . . ." She fumbles with her cigarette. "I wanted him to *think* that we didn't need him, for him to wonder . . ."

"While we went without food?"

She tosses the butt down and grinds it with her foot.

"I think it's out now," I joke. "You're not going to set off a forest fire."

She laughs. She actually laughs at my joke. A novelty. "He never called again, after he left. I phoned him plenty, at all hours; you can imagine."

Yeah, I can imagine.

"At first he took my calls, but once he remarried he got an unlisted number. He moved around the country. He never came back to visit. Just the child-support checks, like clockwork. And now you're eighteen."

"So?"

"They'll stop."

"The checks?"

"Yes. We're no longer his responsibility." She lights another cigarette.

"Don't smoke them all at once."

"Do you have the other checks with you?"

"Yeah."

"You'd better deposit those, then. I'll sign the backs. My checkbook's in the room. Let me just finish my cigarette."

And the presents, I want to say, but there's no need. They *were* from him. But I realize, all of sudden, that it wouldn't have seemed fair to her, for him to be the hero, sending expensive gifts, but not lifting a finger to raise me.

"Maybe I should write to him," I say.

Mom leans her head back and blows smoke into the air. The sky is bright blue. Birds chirp. Clouds float by like pieces of somebody's dream. "Maybe." Mom looks around the courtyard at the other patients. "They only come here to smoke. Not to enjoy the sky. I would like to be a person who enjoys the sky."

"Yeah." Something snaps inside me, and I relax. "Me too."

Walter's last hypothetical question was:

If you were an article of clothing, what would you be?

And I wrote: I would be a brightly colored dress that grows used to its owner's body, clings to her skin, flows with her movements, is soft and forgiving at the waist. I would be that sure of my function, that comfortable with who I am.

AFTERWORD

WRITE WHAT YOU KNOW is advice writing teachers give to students, but it's limiting advice with which I've never agreed.

Still, for the first time, I *have* written what I *know* in this book. I'm not Sage and the characters in *To Be Mona* are fictional, but I did grow up with a bipolar parent. I did live with the embarrassment, uncertainty, and confusion of having the person most central to my well-being be completely erratic and unpredictable.

Bipolar individuals tend to have a high level of intellect and creativity. Abraham Lincoln is suspected to have been bipolar, with his intense energy and crashing depressions. Actress Patty Duke; newscaster Jane Pauley; and psychiatrist Kay Redfield Jamison are bipolar and have written striking memoirs about living with the disease.

Bipolar disorder is biological and treatable with medication. It is also genetic. In my family, several people have been diagnosed with the disease in adulthood. Tragically, one of them committed suicide. Another is trying to "brave it out" without treatment, creating havoc for everyone in his life. Yet another dutifully swallows her medication each day, has her blood levels checked, seeks support, and lives normally as a parent, wife, teacher, and artist.

So you tell me, which is braver?

✗ ✗ ✗ ✗

There are many signs that you (or a friend) are in an abusive relationship. Sage experiences many of these in her relationship with Roger:

✗ You feel you have to "walk on eggshells" and be careful about what you do or say.

✗ You feel discomfort or confusion at a gut level when you are with your partner.

✗ Your partner accuses you of things that are unfair or untrue.

✗ You don't feel that your feelings and needs are noticed or honored.

✗ You don't feel that it's okay to be yourself or express yourself.

✗ Your partner insists that you give up activities or friendships that you enjoy.

He (or she) switches behaviors, leaving you unbalanced.

He (or she) is jealous and possessive.

Your partner threatens you, physically or psychologically.

Your partner makes you responsible for their emotional *well-being*.

✗ ✗ ✗ ✗

The following resources are the tip of the iceberg:

Bipolar Disorder

The Bipolar Disorder Survival Guide by David Miklowitz

An Unquiet Mind by Kay Redfield Jamison

Brilliant Madness: Living with Manic Depressive Illness by Patty Duke and Gloria Hochman

New Hope for Children and Teens with Bipolar Disorder by Boris Birmaher

Skywriting: A Life Out of the Blue by Jane Pauley

✗ ✗ ✗ ✗

Abuse

The Verbally Abusive Relationship: How to Recognize It and How to Respond by Patricia Evans

Codependent No More: How to Stop Controlling Others and Start Caring for Yourself by Melody Beattie

National Coalition Against Domestic Violence: www.ncadv.org

Finally, I want to dedicate this book to all of you who have lived with abuse and mental illness, and struggled to *become*, in spite of it; and to anyone who has been bullied by someone they love.

—Kelly Easton